# The Sword of Welleran

## of Welleran

*and Other Stories*

# The Sword of Welleran

## and Other Stories

### Edward J.M.D. Plunkett, Lord Dunsany

# ÆGYPAN PRESS

*The Sword of Welleran*
*and Other Stories*
A publication of
ÆGYPAN PRESS

www.aegypan.com

# Table of Contents

# The Sword of Welleran

Where the great plain of Tarphet runs up, as the sea in estuaries, among the Cyresian mountains, there stood long since the city of Merimna well-nigh among the shadows of the crags. I have never seen a city in the world so beautiful as Merimna seemed to me when first I dreamed of it. It was a marvel of spires and figures of bronze, and marble fountains, and trophies of fabulous wars, and broad streets given over wholly to the Beautiful. Right through the center of the city there went an avenue fifty strides in width, and along each side of it stood likenesses in bronze of the Kings of all the countries that the people of Merimna had ever known. At the end of that avenue was a colossal chariot with three bronze horses driven by the winged figure of Fame, and behind her in the chariot the huge form of Welleran, Merimna's ancient hero, standing with extended sword. So urgent was the mien and attitude of Fame, and so swift the pose of the horses, that you had sworn that the chariot was instantly upon you, and that its dust already veiled the faces of the Kings. And in the city was a mighty hall wherein were stored the trophies of Merimna's heroes. Sculptured it was and domed, the glory of the art of masons a long while dead, and on the summit of the dome the image of Rollory sat gazing across the Cyresian mountains toward the wide lands beyond, the lands that knew his sword. And beside Rollory, like an old nurse, the figure of Victory sat, hammering into a golden wreath of laurels for his head the crowns of fallen Kings.

Such was Merimna, a city of sculptured Victories and warriors of bronze. Yet in the time of which I write the art of war had been forgotten in Merimna, and the people almost slept. To and fro and up and down they would walk through the marble streets, gazing at memorials of the things achieved by their country's swords in the hands of those that long ago had loved Merimna well. Almost they slept, and dreamed of Welleran, Soorenard, Mommolek, Rollory, Akanax, and young Iraine. Of the lands beyond the mountains that lay all round about them they knew nothing, save that they were the theater of the terrible deeds of Welleran, that he had done with his sword. Long since these lands had fallen back into the possession of the nations that had been scourged by Merimna's armies. Nothing now remained to Merimna's men save their inviolate city and the glory of the remembrance of their ancient fame. At night they would place sentinels far out in the desert, but these always slept at their posts dreaming of Rollory, and three times every night a guard would march around the city clad in purple, bearing lights and singing songs of Welleran. Always the guard went unarmed, but as the sound of their song went echoing across the plain towards the looming mountains, the desert robbers would hear the name of Welleran and steal away to their haunts. Often dawn would come across the plain, shimmering marvelously upon Merimna's spires, abashing all the stars, and find the guard still singing songs of Welleran, and would change the color of their purple robes and pale the lights they bore. But the guard would go back leaving the ramparts safe, and one by one the sentinels in the plain would awake from dreaming of Rollory and shuffle back into the city quite cold. Then something of the menace would pass away from the faces of the Cyresian mountains, that from the north and the west and the south lowered upon Merimna, and clear in the morning the statues and the pillars would arise in the old inviolate city. You would wonder that an unarmed guard and sentinels that slept could defend a city that was stored with all the glories of art, that was rich in gold and bronze, a haughty city that had erst oppressed its neighbors, whose people had forgotten the art of war. Now this is the reason that, though all her other lands had long been taken from her, Merimna's city was safe. A strange thing was believed or feared by the fierce tribes beyond the mountains, and it was credited among them that at certain stations round Merimna's ramparts there still rode Welleran, Soorenard, Mommolek, Rollory, Akanax, and young Iraine. Yet it was close on a hundred years since Iraine, the youngest of Merimna's heroes, fought his last battle with the tribes.

Sometimes indeed there arose among the tribes young men who doubted and said: "How may a man forever escape death?"

But graver men answered them: "Hear us, ye whose wisdom has discerned so much, and discern for us how a man may escape death when two score horsemen assail him with their swords, all of them sworn to kill him, and all of them sworn upon their country's gods; as often Welleran hath. Or discern for us how two men alone may enter a walled city by night, and bring away from it that city's king, as did Soorenard and Mommolek. Surely men that have escaped so many swords and so many sleety arrows shall escape the years and Time."

And the young men were humbled and became silent. Still, the suspicion grew. And often when the sun set on the Cyresian mountains, men in Merimna discerned the forms of savage tribesmen black against the light, peering towards the city.

All knew in Merimna that the figures round the ramparts were only statues of stone, yet even there a hope lingered among a few that some day their old heroes would come again, for certainly none had ever seen them die. Now it had been the wont of these six warriors of old, as each received his last wound and knew it to be mortal, to ride away to a certain deep ravine and cast his body in, as somewhere I have read great elephants do, hiding their bones away from lesser beasts. It was a ravine steep and narrow even at the ends, a great cleft into which no man could come by any path. There rode Welleran alone, panting hard; and there later rode Soorenard and Mommolek, Mommolek with a mortal wound upon him not to return, but Soorenard was unwounded and rode back alone from leaving his dear friend resting among the mighty bones of Welleran. And there rode Soorenard, when his day was come, with Rollory and Akanax, and Rollory rode in the middle and Soorenard and Akanax on either side. And the long ride was a hard and weary thing for Soorenard and Akanax, for they both had mortal wounds; but the long ride was easy for Rollory, for he was dead. So the bones of those five heroes whitened in an enemy's land, and very still they were, though they had troubled cities, and none knew where they lay saving only Iraine, the young captain, who was but twenty-five when Mommolek, Rollory and Akanax rode away. And among them were strewn their saddles and their bridles, and all the accoutrements of their horses, lest any man should ever find them afterwards and say in some foreign city: "Lo! the bridles or the saddles of Merimna's captains, taken in war," but their beloved trusty horses they turned free.

Forty years afterwards, in the hour of a great victory, his last wound came upon Iraine, and the wound was terrible and would not close. And Iraine was the last of the captains, and rode away alone. It was a long way to the dark ravine, and Iraine feared that he would never come to the resting-place of the old heroes, and he urged his horse on swiftly, and clung to the saddle with his hands. And often as he rode he fell asleep, and dreamed of earlier days, and of the times when he first rode forth to the great wars of Welleran, and of the time when Welleran first spake to him, and of the faces of Welleran's comrades when they led charges in the battle. And ever as he awoke a great longing arose in his soul as it hovered on his body's brink, a longing to lie among the bones of the old heroes. At last when he saw the dark ravine making a scar across the plain, the soul of Iraine slipped out through his great wound and spread its wings, and pain departed from the poor hacked body, and, still urging his horse forward, Iraine died. But the old true horse cantered on till suddenly he saw before him the dark ravine and put his forefeet out on the very edge of it and stopped. Then the body of Iraine came toppling forward over the right shoulder of the horse, and his bones mingle and rest as the years go by with the bones of Merimna's heroes.

Now there was a little boy in Merimna named Rold. I saw him first, I, the dreamer, that sit before my fire asleep, I saw him first as his mother led him through the great hall where stand the trophies of Merimna's heroes. He was five years old, and they stood before the great glass casket wherein lay the sword of Welleran, and his mother said: "The sword of Welleran." And

Rold said: "What should a man do with the sword of Welleran?" And his mother answered: "Men look at the sword and remember Welleran." And they went on and stood before the great red cloak of Welleran, and the child said: "Why did Welleran wear this great red cloak?" And his mother answered: "It was the way of Welleran."

When Rold was a little older he stole out of his mother's house quite in the middle of the night when all the world was still, and Merimna asleep dreaming of Welleran, Soorenard, Mommolek, Rollory, Akanax, and young Iraine. And he went down to the ramparts to hear the purple guard go by singing of Welleran. And the purple guard came by with lights, all singing in the stillness, and dark shapes out in the desert turned and fled. And Rold went back again to his mother's house with a great yearning towards the name of Welleran, such as men feel for very holy things.

And in time Rold grew to know the pathway all round the ramparts, and the six equestrian statues that were there guarding Merimna still. These statues were not like other statues, they were so cunningly wrought of many-colored marbles that none might be quite sure until very close that they were not living men. There was a horse of dappled marble, the horse of Akanax. The horse of Rollory was of alabaster, pure white, his armor was wrought out of a stone that shone, and his horseman's cloak was made of a blue stone, very precious. He looked northwards.

But the marble horse of Welleran was pure black, and there sat Welleran upon him looking solemnly westwards. His horse it was whose cold neck Rold most loved to stroke, and it was Welleran whom the watchers at sunset on the mountains the most clearly saw as they peered towards the city. And Rold loved the red nostrils of the great black horse and his rider's jasper cloak.

Now beyond the Cyresians the suspicion grew that Merimna's heroes were dead, and a plan was devised that a man should go by night and come close to the figures upon the ramparts and see whether they were Welleran, Soorenard, Mommolek, Rollory, Akanax, and young Iraine. And all were agreed upon the plan, and many names were mentioned of those who should go, and the plan matured for many years. It was during these years that watchers clustered often at sunset upon the mountains but came no nearer. Finally, a better plan was made, and it was decided that two men who had been by chance condemned to death should be given a pardon if they went down into the plain by night and discovered whether or not Merimna's heroes lived. At first the two prisoners dared not go, but after a while one of them, Seejar, said to his companion, Sajar-Ho: "See now, when the King's axeman smites a man upon the neck that man dies."

And the other said that this was so. Then said Seejar: "And even though Welleran smite a man with his sword no more befalleth him than death."

Then Sajar-Ho thought for a while. Presently he said: "Yet the eye of the King's axeman might err at the moment of his stroke or his arm fail him, and the eye of Welleran hath never erred nor his arm failed. It were better to bide here."

Then said Seejar: "Maybe that Welleran is dead and that some other holds his place upon the ramparts, or even a statue of stone."

But Sajar-Ho made answer: "How can Welleran be dead when he even escaped from two score horsemen with swords that were sworn to slay him, and all sworn upon our country's gods?"

And Seejar said: "This story his father told my grand-father concerning Welleran. On the day that the fight was lost on the plains of Kurlistan he saw a dying horse near to the river, and the horse looked piteously towards the water but could not reach it. And the father of my grandfather saw Welleran go down to the river's brink and bring water from it with his own hand and give it to the horse. Now we are in as sore a plight as was that horse, and as near to death; it may be that Welleran will pity us, while the King's axeman cannot because of the commands of the King."

Then said Sajar-Ho: "Thou wast ever a cunning arguer. Thou broughtest us into this trouble with thy cunning and thy devices, we will see if thou canst bring us out of it. We will go."

So news was brought to the King that the two prisoners would go down to Merimna.

That evening the watchers led them to the mountain's edge, and Seejar and Sajar-Ho went down towards the plain by the way of a deep ravine, and the watchers watched them go. Presently their figures were wholly hid in the dusk. Then night came up, huge and holy, out of waste marshes to the eastwards and low lands and the sea; and the angels that watched over all men through the day closed their great eyes and slept, and the angels that watched over all men through the night awoke and ruffled their deep blue feathers and stood up and watched. But the plain became a thing of mystery filled with fears. So the two spies went down the deep ravine, and coming to the plain sped stealthily across it. Soon they came to the line of sentinels asleep upon the sand, and one stirred in his sleep calling on Rollory, and a great dread seized upon the spies and they whispered "Rollory lives," but they remembered the King's axeman and went on. And next they came to the great bronze statue of Fear, carved by some sculptor of the old glorious years in the attitude of flight towards the mountains, calling to her children as she fled. And the children of Fear were carved in the likeness of the armies of all the trans-Cyresian tribes with their backs towards Merimna, flocking after Fear. And from where he sat on his horse behind the ramparts the sword of Welleran was stretched out over their heads as ever it was wont. And the two spies kneeled down in the sand and kissed the huge bronze foot of the statue of Fear, saying: "O Fear, Fear." And as they knelt they saw lights far off along the ramparts coming nearer and nearer, and heard men singing of Welleran. And the purple guard came nearer and went by with their lights, and passed on into the distance round the ramparts still singing of Welleran. And all the while the two spies clung to the foot of the statue, muttering: "O Fear, Fear." But when they could hear the name of Welleran no more they arose and came to the ramparts and climbed over them and came at once upon the figure of Welleran, and they bowed low to the ground, and Seejar said: "O Welleran, we came to see whether thou didst yet live." And for a long while they waited with their faces to the earth. At last Seejar looked up towards Welleran's terrible sword, and it was still stretched out pointing to the carved armies that followed after Fear. And Seejar bowed to the ground again and touched the horse's hoof, and it seemed cold to him. And he moved his hand higher and touched the leg of the horse, and it seemed quite cold. At last he touched Welleran's foot, and the armor on it seemed hard and stiff. Then as Welleran moved not and spake not, Seejar climbed up at last and touched his hand, the terrible hand of Welleran, and it was marble. Then Seejar laughed aloud, and he and Sajar- Ho sped down the empty pathway and found Rollory, and he was marble too. Then they climbed down over the ramparts and went back across the plain, walking contemptuously past the figure of Fear, and heard the guard returning round the ramparts for the third time, singing of Welleran; and Seejar said: "Aye, you may sing of Welleran, but Welleran is dead and a doom is on your city."

And they passed on and found the sentinel still restless in the night and calling on Rollory. And Sajar-Ho muttered: "Aye, you may call on Rollory, but Rollory is dead and naught can save your city."

And the two spies went back alive to their mountains again, and as they reached them the first ray of the sun came up red over the desert behind Merimna and lit Merimna's spires. It was the hour when the purple guard were wont to go back into the city with their tapers pale and their robes a brighter color, when the cold sentinels came shuffling in from dreaming in the desert; it was the hour when the desert robbers hid themselves away, going back to their mountain caves; it was the hour when gauze-winged insects are born that only live for a day; it was the hour when men die that are condemned to death; and in this hour a great peril, new and terrible, arose for Merimna and Merimna knew it not.

Then Seejar turning said: "See how red the dawn is and how red the spires of Merimna. They are angry with Merimna in Paradise and they bode its doom."

So the two spies went back and brought the news to their King, and for a few days the Kings of those countries were gathering their armies together; and one evening the armies of four Kings were massed together at the top of the deep ravine, all crouching below the summit waiting for the sun to set. All wore resolute and fearless faces, yet inwardly every man was praying to his gods, unto each one in turn.

Then the sun set, and it was the hour when the bats and the dark creatures are abroad and the lions come down from their lairs, and the desert robbers go into the plains again, and fevers rise up winged and hot out of chill marshes, and it was the hour when safety leaves the thrones of Kings, the hour when dynasties change. But in the desert the purple guard came swinging out of Merimna with their lights to sing of Welleran, and the sentinels lay down to sleep.

Now into Paradise no sorrow may ever come, but may only beat like rain against its crystal walls, yet the souls of Merimna's heroes were half aware of some sorrow far away as some sleeper feels that someone is chilled and cold yet knows not in his sleep that it is he. And they fretted a little in their starry home. Then unseen there drifted earthward across the setting sun the souls of Welleran, Soorenard, Mommolek, Rollory, Akanax, and young Iraine. Already when they reached Merimna's ramparts it was just dark, already the armies of the four Kings had begun to move, jingling, down the deep ravine. But when the six warriors saw their city again, so little changed after so many years, they looked towards her with a longing that was nearer to tears than any that their souls had known before, crying to her:

"O Merimna, our city: Merimna, our walled city.

"How beautiful thou art with all thy spires, Merimna. For thee we left the earth, its kingdoms and little flowers, for thee we have come away for awhile from Paradise.

"It is very difficult to draw away from the face of God — it is like a warm fire, it is like dear sleep, it is like a great anthem, yet there is a stillness all about it, a stillness full of lights.

"We have left Paradise for awhile for thee, Merimna.

"Many women have we loved, Merimna, but only one city.

"Behold now all the people dream, all our loved people. How beautiful are dreams! In dreams the dead may live, even the long dead and the very silent. Thy lights are all sunk low, they have all gone out, no sound is in thy streets. Hush! Thou art like a maiden that shutteth up her eyes and is asleep, that draweth her breath softly and is quite still, being at ease and untroubled.

"Behold now the battlements, the old battlements. Do men defend them still as we defended them? They are worn a little, the battlements," and drifting nearer they peered anxiously. "It is not by the hand of man that they are worn, our battlements. Only the years have done it and indomitable Time. Thy battlements are like the girdle of a maiden, a girdle that is round about her. See now the dew upon them, they are like a jeweled girdle.

"Thou art in great danger, Merimna, because thou art so beautiful. Must thou perish tonight because we no more defend thee, because we cry out and none hear us, as the bruised lilies cry out and none have known their voices?"

Thus spake these strong-voiced, battle-ordering captains, calling to their dear city, and their voices came no louder than the whispers of little bats that drift across the twilight in the evening. Then the purple guard came near, going round the ramparts for the first time in the night, and the old warriors called to them, "Merimna is in danger! Already her enemies gather in the darkness." But their voices were never heard because they were only wandering ghosts. And the guard went by and passed unheeding away, still singing of Welleran.

Then said Welleran to his comrades: "Our hands can hold swords no more, our voices cannot be heard, we are stalwart men no longer. We are but dreams, let us go among dreams. Go all of you, and thou too, young Iraine, and trouble the dreams of all the men that sleep, and urge them to take the swords of their grandsires that hang upon the walls, and to gather at the mouth of the ravine; and I will find a leader and make him take my sword."

Then they passed up over the ramparts and into their dear city. And the wind blew about, this way and that, as he went, the soul of Welleran who had upon his day withstood the charges of tempestuous armies. And the souls of his comrades, and with them young Iraine, passed up into the city and troubled the dreams of every man who slept, and to every man the souls said in their dreams: "It is hot and still in the city. Go out now into the desert, but take with thee the old sword that hangs upon the wall for fear of the desert robbers."

And the god of that city sent up a fever over it, and the fever brooded over it and the streets were hot; and all that slept awoke from dreaming that it would be cool and pleasant where the breezes came down the ravine out of the mountains; and they took the old swords that their grandsires had, according to their dreams, for fear of the desert robbers. And in and out of dreams passed the souls of Welleran's comrades, and with them young Iraine, in great haste as the night wore on; and one by one they troubled the dreams of all Merimna's men and caused them to arise and go out armed, all save the purple guard who, heedless of danger, sang of Welleran still, for waking men cannot hear the souls of the dead.

But Welleran drifted over the roofs of the city till he came to the form of Rold lying fast asleep. Now Rold was grown strong and was eighteen years of age, and he was fair of hair and tall like Welleran, and the soul of Welleran hovered over him and went into his dreams as a butterfly flits through trelliswork into a garden of flowers, and the soul of Welleran said to Rold in his dreams: "Thou wouldst go and see again the sword of Welleran, the great curved sword of Welleran. Thou wouldst go and look at it in the night with the moon-light shining upon it."

And the longing of Rold in his dreams to see the sword caused him to walk still sleeping from his mother's house to the hall wherein were the trophies of the heroes. And the soul of Welleran urging the dreams of Rold caused him to pause before the great red cloak, and there the soul said among the dreams: "Thou art cold in the night; fling now a cloak around thee."

And Rold drew round about him the huge red cloak of Welleran. Then Rold's dreams took him to the sword, and the soul said to the dreams: "Thou hast a longing to hold the sword of Welleran: take up the sword in thy hand."

But Rold said: "What should a man do with the sword of Welleran?"

And the soul of the old captain said to the dreamer: "It is a good sword to hold: take up the sword of Welleran."

And Rold, still sleeping and speaking aloud, said: "It is not lawful; none may touch the sword."

And Rold turned to go. Then a great and terrible cry arose in the soul of Welleran, all the more bitter for that he could not utter it, and it went round and round his soul finding no utterance, like a cry evoked long since by some murderous deed in some old haunted chamber that whispers through the ages heard by none.

And the soul of Welleran cried out to the dreams of Rold: "Thy knees are tied! Thou art fallen in a marsh! Thou canst not move."

And the dreams of Rold said to him: "Thy knees are tied, thou art fallen in a marsh," and Rold stood still before the sword. Then the soul of the warrior wailed among Rold's dreams, as Rold stood before the sword.

"Welleran is crying for his sword, his wonderful curved sword. Poor Welleran, that once fought for Merimna, is crying for his sword in the night. Thou wouldst not keep Welleran without his beautiful sword when he is dead and cannot come for it, poor Welleran who fought for Merimna."

And Rold broke the glass casket with his hand and took the sword, the great curved sword of Welleran; and the soul of the warrior said among Rold's dreams: "Welleran is waiting in the deep ravine that runs into the mountains, crying for his sword."

And Rold went down through the city and climbed over the ramparts, and walked with his eyes wide open but still sleeping over the desert to the mountains.

Already a great multitude of Merimna's citizens were gathered in the desert before the deep ravine with old swords in their hands, and Rold passed through them as he slept holding the sword of Welleran, and the people cried in amaze to one another as he passed: "Rold hath the sword of Welleran!"

And Rold came to the mouth of the ravine, and there the voices of the people woke him. And Rold knew nothing that he had done in his sleep, and looked in amazement at the sword in his hand and said: "What art thou, thou beautiful thing? Lights shimmer in thee, thou art restless. It is the sword of Welleran, the curved sword of Welleran!"

And Rold kissed the hilt of it, and it was salt upon his lips with the battle-sweat of Welleran. And Rold said: "What should a man do with the sword of Welleran?"

And all the people wondered at Rold as he sat there with the sword in his hand muttering, "What should a man do with the sword of Welleran?"

Presently there came to the ears of Rold the noise of a jingling up in the ravine, and all the people, the people that knew naught of war, heard the jingling coming nearer in the night; for the four armies were moving on Merimna and not yet expecting an enemy. And Rold gripped upon the hilt of the great curved sword, and the sword seemed to lift a little. And a new thought came into the hearts of Merimna's people as they gripped their grandsires' swords. Nearer and nearer came the heedless armies of the four Kings, and old ancestral memories began to arise in the minds of Merimna's people in the desert with their swords in their hands sitting behind Rold. And all the sentinels were awake holding their spears, for Rollory had put their dreams to flight, Rollory that once could put to flight armies and now was but a dream struggling with other dreams.

And now the armies had come very near. Suddenly Rold leaped up, crying: "Welleran! And the sword of Welleran!" And the savage, lusting sword that had thirsted for a hundred years went up with the hand of Rold and swept through a tribesman's ribs. And with the warm blood all about it there came a joy into the curved soul of that mighty sword, like to the joy of a swimmer coming up dripping out of warm seas after living for long in a dry land. When they saw the red cloak and that terrible sword a cry ran through the tribal armies, "Welleran lives!" And there arose the sounds of exulting of victorious men, and the panting of those that fled, and the sword singing softly to itself as it whirled dripping through the air. And the last that I saw of the battle as it poured into the depth and darkness of the ravine was the sword of Welleran sweeping up and falling, gleaming blue in the moonlight whenever it arose and afterwards gleaming red, and so disappearing into the darkness.

But in the dawn Merimna's men came back, and the sun arising to give new life to the world, shone instead upon the hideous things that the sword of Welleran had done. And Rold said: "O sword, sword! How horrible thou art! Thou art a terrible thing to have come among men. How many eyes shall look upon gardens no more because of thee? How many fields must go empty that might have been fair with cottages, white cottages with children all about them? How many valleys must go desolate that might have nursed warm hamlets, because thou hast slain long since the men that might have built them? I hear the wind crying against thee, thou sword! It comes from the empty valleys. It comes over the bare fields. There are children's voices in it. They were never born. Death brings an end to crying for those that had life once, but these must cry forever. O sword! sword! why did the gods send thee among men?" And the tears of Rold fell down upon the proud sword but could not wash it clean.

And now that the ardor of battle had passed away, the spirits of Merimna's people began to gloom a little, like their leader's, with their fatigue and with the cold of the morning; and they looked at the sword of Welleran in Rold's hand and said: "Not anymore, not anymore forever will Welleran now return, for his sword is in the hand of another. Now we know indeed that he is dead. O Welleran, thou wast our sun and moon and all our stars. Now is the sun fallen down and the moon broken, and all the stars are scattered as the diamonds of a necklace that is snapped off one who is slain by violence."

Thus wept the people of Merimna in the hour of their great victory, for men have strange moods, while beside them their old inviolate city slumbered safe. But back from the ramparts and beyond the mountains and over the lands that they had conquered of old, beyond the world and back again to Paradise, went the souls of Welleran, Soorenard, Mommolek, Rollory, Akanax, and young Iraine.

# The Fall of Babbulkund

*I* said: "I will arise now and see Babbulkund, City of Marvel. She is of one age with the earth; the stars are her sisters. Pharaohs of the old time coming conquering from Araby first saw her, a solitary mountain in the desert, and cut the mountain into towers and terraces. They destroyed one of the hills of God, but they made Babbulkund. She is carven, not built; her palaces are one with her terraces, there is neither join nor cleft. Hers is the beauty of the youth of the world. She deemeth herself to be the middle of Earth, and hath four gates facing outward to the Nations. There sits outside her eastern gate a colossal god of stone. His face flushes with the lights of dawn. When the morning sunlight warms his lips they part a little, and he giveth utterance to the words 'Oon Oom,' and the language is long since dead in which he speaks, and all his worshippers are gathered to their tombs, so that none knoweth what the words portend that he uttereth at dawn. Some say that he greets the sun as one god greeets another in the language thereof, and others say that he proclaims the day, and others that he uttereth warning.

And at every gate is a marvel not credible until beholden."

And I gathered three friends and said to them: "We are what we have seen and known. Let us journey now and behold Babbulkund, that our minds may be beautified with it and our spirits made holier."

So we took ship and traveled over the lifting sea, and remembered not things done in the towns we knew, but laid away the thoughts of them like soiled linen and put them by, and dreamed of Babbulkund.

But when we came to the land of which Babbulkund is the abiding glory, we hired a caravan of camels and Arab guides, and passed southwards in the afternoon on the three days' journey through the desert that should bring us to the white walls of Babbulkund. And the heat of the sun shone upon us out of the bright grey sky, and the heat of the desert beat up at us from below.

About sunset we halted and tethered our horses, while the Arabs unloaded the provisions from the camels and prepared a fire out of the dry scrub, for at sunset the heat of the desert departs from it suddenly, like a bird. Then we saw a traveler approaching us on a camel coming from the south. When he was come near we said to him:

"Come and encamp among us, for in the desert all men are brothers, and we will give thee meat to eat and wine, or, if thou art bound by thy faith, we will give thee some other drink that is not accursed by the prophet."

The traveler seated himself beside us on the sand, and crossed his legs and answered:

"Hearken, and I will tell you of Babbulkund, City of Marvel. Babbulkund stands just below the meeting of the rivers, where Oonrana, River of Myth, flows into the Waters of Fable, even the old stream Plegáthanees.

These, together, enter her northern gate rejoicing. Of old they flowed in the dark through the Hill that Nehemoth, the first of Pharaohs, carved into the City of Marvel. Sterile and desolate they float far through the desert, each in the appointed cleft, with life upon neither bank, but give birth in Babbulkund to the sacred purple garden whereof all nations sing. Thither all the bees come on a pilgrimage at evening by a secret way of the air. Once, from his twilit kingdom, which he rules equally with the sun, the moon saw and loved Babbulkund, clad with her purple garden; and the moon wooed Babbulkund, and she sent him weeping away, for she is more beautiful than all her sisters the stars. Her sisters come to her at night into her maiden chamber. Even the gods speak sometimes of Babbulkund, clad with her purple garden. Listen, for I perceive by your eyes that ye have not seen Babbulkund; there is a restlessness in them and an unappeased wonder. Listen. In the garden whereof I spoke there is a lake that hath no twin or fellow in the world; there is no companion for it among all the lakes. The shores of it are of glass, and the bottom of it. In it are great fish having golden and scarlet scales, and they swim to and fro. Here it is the wont of the eighty-second Nehemoth (who rules in the city today) to come, after the dusk has fallen, and sit by the lake alone, and at this hour eight hundred slaves go down by steps through caverns into vaults beneath the lake. Four hundred of them carrying purple lights march one behind the other, from east to west, and four hundred carrying green lights march one behind the other, from west to east. The two lines cross and re-cross each other in and out as the slaves go round and round, and the fearful fish flash up and down and to and fro."

But upon that traveler speaking night descended, solemn and cold, and we wrapped ourselves in our blankets and lay down upon the sand in the sight of the astral sisters of Babbulkund. And all that night the desert said many things, softly and in a whisper, but I knew not what he said. Only the sand knew and arose and was troubled and lay down again, and the wind knew. Then, as the hours of the night went by, these two discovered the foot-tracks wherewith we had disturbed the holy desert, and they troubled over them and covered them up; and then the wind lay down and the sand rested. Then the wind arose again and the sand danced. This they did many times. And all the while the desert whispered what I shall not know.

Then I slept awhile and awoke just before sunrise, very cold. Suddenly the sun leapt up and flamed upon our faces; we all threw off our blankets and stood up. Then we took food, and afterwards started southwards, and in the heat of the day rested, and afterwards pushed on again. And all the while the desert remained the same, like a dream that will not cease to trouble a tired sleeper.

And often travelers passed us in the desert, coming from the City of Marvel, and there was a light and a glory in their eyes from having seen Babbulkund.

That evening, at sunset, another traveler neared us, and we hailed him, saying:

"Wilt thou eat and drink with us, seeing that all men are brothers in the desert?"

And he descended from his camel and sat by us and said:

"When morning shines on the colossus Neb and Neb speaks, at once the musicians of King Nehemoth in Babbulkund awake.

"At first their fingers wander over their golden harps, or they stroke idly their violins. Clearer and clearer the note of each instrument ascends like larks arising from the dew, till suddenly they all blend together and a new melody is born. Thus, every morning, the musicians of King Nehemoth make a new marvel in the City of Marvel; for these are no common musicians, but masters of melody, raided by conquest long since, and carried away in ships from the Isles of Song. And, at the sound of the music, Nehemoth awakes in the eastern chamber of his palace, which is carved in the form of a great crescent, four miles long, on the northern side of the city. Full in the windows of its eastern chamber the sun rises, and full in the windows of its western chamber the sun sets.

"When Nehemoth awakes he summons slaves who bring a palanquin with bells, which the King enters, having lightly robed. Then the slaves run and bear him to the onyx Chamber of the Bath, with the sound of small bells ringing as they run. And when Nehemoth emerges thence, bathed and anointed, the slaves run on with their ringing palanquin and bear him to the Orient Chamber of Banquets, where the King takes the first meal of the day. Thence, through the great white corridor whose windows all face sunwards, Nehemoth, in his palanquin, passes on to the Audience Chamber of Embassies from the North, which is all decked wim Northern wares.

"All about it are ornaments of amber from the North and carven chalices of the dark brown Northern crystal, and on its floors lie furs from Baltic shores.

"In adjoining chambers are stored the wonted food of the hardy Northern men, and the strong wine of the North, pale but terrible. Therein the King receives barbarian princes from the frigid lands. Thence the slaves bear him swiftly to the Audience Chamber of Embassies from the East, where the walls are of turquoise, studded with the rubies of Ceylon, where the gods are the gods of the East, where all the hangings have been devised in the gorgeous heart of Ind, and where all the carvings have been wrought with the cunning of the isles. Here, if a caravan hath chanced to have come in from Ind or from Cathay, it is the King's wont to converse awhile with Moguls or Mandarins, for from the East come the arts and knowledge of the world, and the converse of their people is polite. Thus Nehemoth passes on through the other Audience Chambers and receives, perhaps, some Sheikhs of the Arab folk who have crossed the great desert from me West, or receives an embassy sent to do him homage from the shy jungle people to the South. And all the while the slaves with the ringing palanquin run westwards, following the sun, and ever the sun shines straight into the chamber where Nehemoth sits, and all the while the music from one or other of his bands of musicians comes tinkling to his ears. But when the middle of the day draws near, the slaves run to the cool groves that lie along the verandahs on me northern side of the palace, forsaking the sun, and as the heat overcomes the genius of the musicians, one by one their hands fall from their instruments, till at last all melody ceases. At this moment Nehemoth falls asleep, and the slaves put the palanquin down and lie down beside it. At this hour the city becomes quite still, and the palace of Nehemoth and the tombs of the Pharaohs of old face to the sunlight, all alike in silence. Even the jewelers in the marketplace, selling gems to princes, cease from their bargaining and cease to sing; for in Babbulkund the vendor of rubies sings the song of the ruby, and the vendor of sapphires sings the song of the sapphire, and each stone hath its song, so that a man, by his song, proclaims and makes known his wares.

"But all these sounds cease at the meridian hour, the jewelers in the marketplace lie down in what shadow they can find, and the princes go back to the cool places in their palaces, and a great hush in the gleaming air hangs over Babbulkund. But in the cool of the late afternoon, one of the King's musicians will awake from dreaming of his home and will pass his fingers, perhaps, over the strings of his harp and, with the music, some memory may arise of the wind in the glens of the mountains that stand in the Isles of Song. Then the musician will wrench great cries out of the soul of his harp for the sake of the old memory, and his fellows will awake and all make a song of home, woven of sayings told in the harbor when the ships came in, and of tales in the cottages about the people of old time. One by one the other bands of musicians will take up the song, and Babbulkund, City of Marvel, will throb with this marvel anew. Just now Nehemoth awakes, the slaves leap to their feet and bear the palanquin to the outer side of the great crescent palace between the south and the west, to behold the sun again. The palanquin, with its ringing bells, goes round once more; the voices of the jewelers sing again, in the marketplace, the song of the emerald, the song of the sapphire; men talk on the housetops, beggars wail in the streets, the musicians bend to their work, all the sounds blend together into one murmur, the voice of Babbulkund speaking at evening. Lower and lower sinks the sun, till Nehemoth, following it, comes with his panting slaves to the great purple garden of which surely thine own country has its songs, from wherever thou art come.

"There he alights from his palanquin and goes up to a throne of ivory set in the garden's midst, facing full westwards, and sits there alone, long regarding the sunlight until it is quite gone. At this hour trouble comes into the face of Nehemoth. Men have heard him muttering at the time of sunset: 'Even I too, even I too.' Thus do King Nehemoth and the sun make their glorious ambits about Babbulkund.

"A little later, when the stars come out to envy the beauty of the City of Marvel, the King walks to another part of the garden and sits in an alcove of opal all alone by the marge of the sacred lake. This is the lake whose shores and floors are of glass, which is lit from beneath by slaves with purple lights and with green lights intermingling, and is one of the seven wonders of Babbulkund. Three of the wonders are in the city's midst and four are at her gates. There is the lake, of which I tell thee, and the purple garden of which I have told thee and which is a wonder even to the stars, and there is Ong Zwarba, of which I shall tell thee also. And the wonders at the gates are these. At the eastern gate Neb. And at the northern gate the wonder of the river and the arches, for the River of Myth, which becomes one with the Waters of Fable in the desert outside the city, floats under a gate of pure gold, rejoicing, and under many arches fantastically carven that are one with either bank. The marvel at the western gate is the marvel of Annolith and the dog Voth. Annolith sits outside the western gate facing towards the city. He is higher than any of the towers or palaces, for his head was carved from the summit of the old hill; he hath two eyes of sapphire wherewith he regards Babbulkund, and the wonder of the eyes is that they are today in the same sockets wherein they glowed when first the world began, only the marble that covered them has been carven away and the light of day let in and the sight of the envious stars. Larger than a lion is the dog Voth beside him; every hair is carven upon the back of Voth, his war hackles are erected and his teeth are bared. All the Nehemoths have worshipped the god Annolith, but all their people pray to the dog Voth, for the law of the land is that none but a Nehemoth may worship the god Annolith. The marvel at the southern gate is the marvel of the jungle, for he comes with all his wild untraveled sea of darkness and trees and tigers and sunward-aspiring orchids right through a marble gate in the city wall and enters the city, and there widens and holds a space in its midst of many miles across. Moreover, he is older than the City of Marvel, for he dwelt long since in one of the valleys of the mountain which Nehemoth, first of Pharaohs, carved into Babbulkund.

"Now the opal alcove in which the King sits at evening by the lake stands at the edge of the jungle, and the climbing orchids of the jungle have long since crept from their homes through clefts of the opal alcove, lured by the lights of the lake, and now bloom there exultingly. Near to this alcove are the harems of Nehemoth.

"The King hath four harems — one for the stalwart women from the mountains to the north, one for the dark and furtive jungle women, one for the desert women that have wandering souls and pine in Babbulkund, and one for the princesses of his own kith, whose brown cheeks blush with the blood of ancient Pharaohs and who exult with Babbulkund in her surpassing beauty, and who know naught of the desert or the jungle or the bleak hills to the north. Quite unadorned and clad in simple garments go all the kith of Nehemoth, for they know well that he grows weary of pomp. Unadorned all save one, the Princess Linderith, who weareth Ong Zwarba and the three lesser gems of the sea. Such a stone is Ong Zwarba that there are none like it even in the turban of Nehemoth nor in all the sanctuaries of the sea. The same god that made Linderith made long ago Ong Zwarbaj; she and Ong Zwarba shine together with one light, and beside this marvelous stone gleam the three lesser ones of the sea.

"Now when the King sitteth in his opal alcove by the sacred lake with the orchids blooming around him all sounds are become still. The sound of the tramping of the weary slaves as they go round and round never comes to the surface. Long since the musicians sleep, and their hands have fallen dumb upon their instruments, and the voices in the city have died away. Perhaps a sigh of one of the desert women has become half a song, or on a hot night in summer one of the women of the hills sings softly a song of snow; all night long in the midst of the purple garden sings one nightingale; all else is still; the stars that look on Babhulkund arise and set, the cold unhappy moon drifts lonely through them, the night wears on; at last the dark figure of Nehemoth, eighty-second of his line, rises and moves stealthily away."

The traveler ceased to speak. For a long time the clear stars, sisters of Babbulkund, had shone upon him speaking, the desert wind had arisen and whispered to the sand, and the sand had long gone secretly to and fro; none of us had moved, none of us had fallen asleep, not so much from wonder at his tale as from the thought that we ourselves in two days' time should see that wondrous city. Then we wrapped our blankets around us and lay down with our feet towards the embers of our fire and instantly were asleep, and in our dreams we multiplied the fame of the City of Marvel.

The sun arose and flamed upon our faces, and all the desert glinted with its light. Then we stood up and prepared the morning meal, and, when we had eaten, the traveler departed. And we commended his soul to the god of the land whereto he went, of the land of his home to the northward, and he commended our souls to the God of the people of the land wherefrom we had come. Then a traveler overtook us going on foot; he wore a brown cloak that was all in rags and he seemed to have been walking all night, and he walked hurriedly but appeared weary, so we offered him food and drink, of which he partook thankfully. When we asked him where he was going, he answered "Babbulkund." Then we offered him a camel upon which to ride, for we said, "We also go to Babbulkund." But he answered strangely:

"Nay, pass on before me, for it is a sore thing never to have seen Babbulkund, having lived while yet she stood. Pass on before me and behold her, and then flee away at once, returning northwards."

Then, though we understood him not, we left him, for he was insistent, and passed on our journey southwards through the desert, and we came before the middle of the day to an oasis of palm trees standing by a well and there we gave water to the haughty camels and replenished our water-bottles and soothed our eyes with the sight of green things and tarried for many hours in the shade. Some of the men slept, but of those that remained awake each man sang softly the songs of his own country, telling of Babbulkund. When the afternoon was far spent we traveled a little way southwards, and went on through the cool evening until the sun fell low and we encamped, and as we sat in our encampment the man in rags overtook us, having traveled all the day, and we gave him food and drink again, and in the twilight he spoke, saying:

"I am the servant of the Lord the God of my people, and I go to do his work on Babbulkund. She is the most beautiful city in the world; there hath been none like her, even the stars of God go envious of her beauty. She is all white, yet with streaks of pink that pass through her streets and houses like flames in the white mind of a sculptor, like desire in Paradise. She hath been carved of old out of a holy hill, no slaves wrought the City of Marvel, but artists toiling at the work they loved. They took no pattern from the houses of men, but each man wrought what his inner eye had seen and carved in marble the visions of his dream. Allover the roof of one of the palace chambers winged lions flit like bats, the size of every one is the size of the lions of God, and the wings are larger than any wing created; they are one above the other more than a man can number, they are all carven out of one block of marble, the chamber itself is hollowed from it, and it is borne aloft upon the carven branches of a grove of clustered tree-ferns wrought by the hand of some jungle mason that loved the tall fern well. Over the River of Myth, which is one with the Waters of Fable, go bridges, fashioned like the wisteria tree and like the drooping laburnum, and a hundred others of wonderful devices, the desire of the souls of masons a long while dead. Oh! very beautiful is white Babbulkund, very beautiful she is, but proud; and the Lord the God of my people hath seen her in her pride, and looking towards her hath seen the prayers of Nehemoth going up to the abomination Annolith and all the people following after Voth. She is very beautiful, Babbulkund; alas, that I may not bless her. I could live always on one of her inner terraces looking on the mysterious jungle in her midst and the heavenward faces of the orchids that, clambering from the darkness, behold the sun. I could love Babbulkund with a great love, yet am I the servant of the Lord the God of my people, and the King hath sinned unto the abomination Annolith, and the people lust exceedingly for Voth. Alas for thee, Babbulkund, alas that I may not even now turn back, for tomorrow I must prophesy against thee and cry out against thee, Babbulkund. But ye travelers that have entreated me hospitably, rise and pass on with your camels, for I can tarry no longer, and I go to do the work on Babbulkund of the Lord the God of my people. Go now and see the beauty of Babbulkund before I cry out against her, and then flee swiftly northwards."

A smoldering fragment fell in upon our campfire and sent a strange light into the eyes of the man in rags. He rose at once, and his tattered cloak swirled up with him like a great wing; he said no more, but turned round from us instantly southwards, and strode away into the darkness towards Babbulkund. Then a hush fell upon our encampment, and the smell of the tobacco of those lands arose. When the last flame died down in our campfire I fell asleep, but my rest was troubled by shifting dreams of doom.

Morning came, and our guides told us that we should come to the city ere nightfall. Again we passed southwards through the changeless desert; sometimes we met travelers coming from Babbulkund, with the beauty of its marvels still fresh in their eyes.

When we encamped near the middle of the day we saw a great number of people on foot coming towards us running, from the southwards. These we hailed when they were come near, saying, "What of Babbulkund?"

They answered: "We are not of the race of the people of Babbulkund, but were captured in youth and taken away from the hills that are to the northward. Now we have all seen in visions of the stillness the Lord the God of our people calling to us from His hills, and therefore we all flee northwards. But in Babbulkund King Nehemoth hath been troubled in the nights by unkingly dreams of doom, and none may interpret what the dreams portend. Now this is the dream that King Nehemoth dreamed on the first night of his dreaming. He saw move through the stillness a bird all black, and beneath the beatings of his wings Babbulkund gloomed and darkened; and after him flew a bird all white, beneath the beatings of whose wings

Babbulkund gleamed and shone; and there flew by four more birds alternately black and white. And, as the black ones passed Babbulkund darkened, and when the white ones appeared her streets and houses shone. But after the sixth bird there came no more, and Babbulkund vanished from her place, and there was only the empty desert where she had stood, and the rivers Oonrana and Plegáthanees mourning alone. Next morning all the prophets of the King gathered before their abominations and questioned them of the dream, and the abominations spake not. But when the second night stepped down from the halls of God, dowered with many stars, King Nehemoth dreamed again; and in this dream King Nehemoth saw four birds only, black and white alternately as before. And Babbulkund darkened again as the black ones passed, and shone when the white came by; only after the four birds came no more, and Babbulkund vanished from her place, leaving only the forgetful desert and the mourning rivers.

"Still the abominations spake not, and none could interpret the dream. And when the third night came forth from the divine halls of her home dowered like her sisters, again King Nehemoth dreamed. And he saw a bird all black go by again, beneath whom Babbulkund darkened, and then a white bird and Babbulkund shone; and after them came no more, and Babbulkund passed away. And the golden day appeared, dispelling dreams, and still the abominations were silent, and the King's prophets answered not to portend the omen of the dream. One prophet only spake before the King, saying: 'The sable birds, O King, are the nights, and the white birds are the days . . .' This thing the King had feared, and he arose and smote the prophet with his sword, whose soul went crying away and had to do no more with nights and days.

"It was last night that the King dreamed his third dream, and this morning we fled away from Bab-bulkund. A great heat lies over it, and the orchids of the jungle droop their heads. All night long the women in the harem of the North have wailed horribly for their hills. A fear hath fallen upon the city, and a boding. Twice hath Nehemoth gone to worship Anno-lith, and all the people have prostrated themselves before Voth. Thrice the horologers have looked into the great crystal globe wherein are foretold all happenings to be, and thrice the globe was blank. Yea, though they went a fourth time yet was no vision revealed; and the people's voice is hushed in Babbulkund."

Soon the travelers arose and pushed on northwards again, leaving us wondering. Through the heat of the day we rested as well as we might, but the air was motionless and sultry and the camels ill at ease. The Arabs said that it boded a desert storm, and that a great wind would arise full of sand. So we arose in the afternoon, and traveled swiftly, hoping to come to shelter before the storm. And the air burned in the stillness between the baked desert and the glaring sky.

Suddenly a wind arose out of the South, blowing from Babbulkund, and the sand lifted and went by in great shapes, all whispering. And the wind blew violently, and wailed as it blew, and hundreds of sandy shapes went towering by, and there were little cries among them and the sounds of a passing away. Soon the wind sank quite suddenly, and its cries died, and the panic ceased among the driven sands. And when the storm departed the air was cool, and the terrible sultriness and the boding were passed away, and the camels had ease among them. And the Arabs said that the storm which was to be had been, as was willed of old by God.

The sun set and the gloaming came, and we neared the junction of Oonrana and Plegáthanees, but in the darkness discerned not Babbulkund. We pushed on hurriedly to reach the city ere nightfall, and came to the junction of the River of Myth where he meets with the Waters of Fable, and still saw not Babbulkund. All round us lay the sand and rocks of the unchanging desert, save to the southwards where the jungle stood with its orchids facing skywards. Then we perceived that we had arrived too late, and that her doom had come to Babbulkund; and by the river in the empty desert on the sand the man in rags was seated, with his face hidden in his hands, weeping bitterly.

*T*hus passed away in the hour of her iniquities before Annolith, in the two thousand and thirty-second year of her being, in the six thousand and fiftieth year of the building of the World, Babbulkund, City of Marvel, sometime called by those that hated her City of the Dog, but hourly mourned in Araby and Ind and wide through jungle and desert; leaving no memorial in stone to show that she had been, but remembered with an abiding love, in spite of the anger of God, by all that knew her beauty, whereof still they sing.

# The Kith of the Elf Folk

## Chapter I

The north wind was blowing, and red and golden the last days of Autumn were streaming hence. Solemn and cold over the marshes arose the evening.

It became very still.

Then the last pigeon went home to the trees on the dry land in the distance, whose shapes already had taken upon themselves a mystery in the haze.

Then all was still again.

As the light faded and the haze deepened, mystery crept nearer from every side.

Then the green plover came in crying, and all alighted.

And again it became still, save when one of the plover rose and flew a little way uttering the cry of the waste. And hushed and silent became the earth, expecting the first star. Then the duck came in, and the widgeon, company by company: and all the light of day faded out of the sky saving one red band of light. Across the light appeared, black and huge, the wings of a flock of geese beating up wind to the marshes. These too went down among the rushes.

Then the stars appeared and shone in the stillness, and there was silence in the great spaces of the night.

Suddenly the bells of the cathedral in the marshes broke out, calling to evensong.

Eight centuries ago on the edge of the marsh men had built the huge cathedral, or it may have been seven centuries ago, or perhaps nine — it was all one to the Wild Things.

So evensong was held, and candles lighted, and the lights through the windows shone red and green in the water, and the sound of the organ, went roaring over the marshes. But from the deep and perilous places, edged with bright mosses, the Wild Things came leaping up to dance on the reflection of the stars, and over their heads as they danced the marsh-lights rose and fell.

The Wild Things are somewhat human in appearance, only all brown of skin and barely two feet high. Their ears are pointed like the squirrel's, only far larger, and they leap to prodigious heights. They live all day under deep pools in the loneliest marshes, but at night they come up and dance. Each Wild Thing has over its head a marsh-light, which moves as the Wild Thing moves; they have no souls, and cannot die, and are of the kith of the Elf-folk.

All night they dance over the marshes, treading upon the reflection of the stars (for the bare surface of the water will not hold them by itself); but when the stars begin to pale, they sink down one by one into the pools of their home. Or if they tarry longer, sitting upon the rushes, their bodies fade from view as the marsh-fires pale in the light, and by daylight none may see the Wild Things of the kith of the Elf-folk. Neither may any see them even at night unless they were born, as I was, in the hour of dusk, just at the moment when the first star appears.

Now, on the night that I tell of, a little Wild Thing had gone drifting over the waste, till it came right up to the walls of the cathedral and danced upon the images of the colored saints as they lay in the water among the reflection of the stars. And as it leaped in its fantastic dance, it saw through the painted windows to where the people prayed, and heard the organ roaring over the marshes. The sound of the organ roared over the marshes, but the song and prayers of the people streamed up from the cathedral's highest tower like thin gold chains, and reached to Paradise, and up and down them went the angels from Paradise to the people, and from the people to Paradise again.

Then something akin to discontent troubled the Wild Thing for the first time since the making of the marshes; and the soft grey ooze and the chill of the deep water seemed to be not enough, nor the first arrival from northwards of the tumultuous geese, nor the wild rejoicing of the wings of the wildfowl when every feather sings, nor the wonder of the calm ice that comes when the snipe depart and beards the rushes with frost and clothes the hushed waste with a mysterious haze where the sun goes red and low, nor even the dance of the Wild Things in the marvelous night; and the little Wild Thing longed to have a soul, and to go and worship God.

And when evensong was over and the lights were out, it went back crying to its kith.

But on the next night, as soon as the images of the stars appeared in the water, it went leaping away from star to star to the farthest edge of the marshlands, where a great wood grew where dwelt the Oldest of the Wild Things.

And it found the Oldest of Wild Things sitting under a tree, sheltering itself from the moon.

And the little Wild Thing said: "I want to have a soul to worship God, and to know the meaning of music, and to see the inner beauty of the marshlands and to imagine Paradise."

And the Oldest of the Wild Things said to it: "What have we to do with God? We are only Wild Things, and of the kith of the Elf-folk."

But it only answered, "I want to have a soul."

Then the Oldest of the Wild Things said: "I have no soul to give you; but if you got a soul, one day you would have to die, and if you knew the meaning of music you would learn the meaning of sorrow, and it is better to be a Wild Thing and not to die."

So it went weeping away.

But they that were kin to the Elf-folk were sorry for the little Wild Thing; and though the Wild Things cannot sorrow long, having no souls to sorrow with, yet they felt for awhile a soreness where their souls should be, when they saw the grief of their comrade.

So the kith of the Elf-folk went abroad by night to make a soul for the little Wild Thing. And they went over the marshes till they came to the high fields among the flowers and grasses. And there they gathered a large piece of gossamer that the spider had laid by twilight; and the dew was on it.

Into this dew had shone all the lights of the long banks of the ribbed sky, as all the colors changed in the restful spaces of evening. And over it the marvelous night had gleamed with all its stars.

Then the Wild Things went with their dew-bespan-gled gossamer down to the edge of their home. And there they gathered a piece of the grey mist that lies by night over the marshlands. And into it they put the melody of the waste that is borne up and down the marshes in the evening on the wings of the golden plover. And they put into it too the mournful song that the reeds are compelled to sing before the presence of the arrogant North Wind. Then each of the Wild Things gave some treasured memory of the old marshes, "For we can spare it," they said. And to all this they added a few images of the stars that they gathered out of the water. Still the soul that the kith of the Elf-folk were making had no life.

Then they put into it the low voices of two lovers that went walking in the night, wandering late alone. And after that they waited for the dawn. And the queenly dawn appeared, and the marsh-lights of the Wild Things paled in the glare, and their bodies faded from view; and still they waited by the marsh's edge. And to them waiting came over field and marsh, from the ground and out of the sky, the myriad song of the birds.

This too the Wild Things put into the piece of haze that they had gathered in the marshlands, and wrapped it all up in their dew-bespangled gossamer. Then the soul lived. And there it lay in the hands of the Wild Things no larger than a hedgehog; and wonderful lights were in it, green and blue; and they changed ceaselessly, going round and round; and in the grey midst of it was a purple flare. And the next night they came to the little Wild Thing and showed her the gleaming soul. And they said to her: "If you must have a soul and go and worship God, and become a mortal and die, place this to your left breast a little above the heart, and it will enter and you will become a human. But if you take it you can never be rid of it to become immortal again unless you pluck it out and give it to another; and we will not take it, and most of the humans have a soul already. And if you cannot find a human without a soul you will one day die, and your soul cannot go to Paradise, because it was only made in the marshes." Far away the little Wild Thing saw the cathedral windows alight for evensong, and the song of the people mounting up to Paradise, and all the angels going up and down. So it bid farewell with tears and thanks to the Wild Things of the kith of Elf-folk, and went leaping away towards the green dry land, holding the soul in its hands.

And the Wild Things were sorry that it had gone, but could not be sorry long, because they had no souls. At the marsh's edge the little Wild Thing gazed for some moments over the water to where the marsh-fires were leaping up and down, and then pressed the soul against its left breast a little above the heart. Instantly it became a young and beautiful woman, who was cold and frightened. She clad herself somehow with bundles of reeds, and went towards the lights of a house that stood close by. And she pushed open the door and entered, and found a farmer and a farmer's wife sitting over their supper.

And the farmer's wife took the little Wild Thing with the soul of the marshes up to her room, and clothed her and braided her hair, and brought her down again, and gave her the first food that she had ever eaten. Then the farmer's wife asked many questions.

"Where have you come from?" she said.

"Over the marshes."

"From what direction?" said the farmer's wife.

"South," said the little Wild Thing with the new soul.

"But none can come over the marshes from the south," said the farmer's wife.

"No, they can't do that," said the farmer.

"I lived in the marshes."

"Who are you?" asked the farmer's wife.

"I am a Wild Thing, and have found a soul in the marshes, and we are kin to the Elf-folk."

Talking it over afterwards, the farmer and his wife agreed that she must be a gypsy who had been lost, and that she was queer with hunger and exposure.

So that night the little Wild Thing slept in the farmer's house, but her new soul stayed awake the whole night long dreaming of the beauty of the marshes.

As soon as dawn came over the waste and shone on the farmer's house, she looked from the window towards the glittering waters, and saw the inner beauty of the marsh. For the Wild Things only love the marsh and know its haunts, but now she perceived the mystery of its distances and the glamour of its perilous pools, with their fair and deadly mosses, and felt the marvel of the North Wind who comes dominant out of unknown icy lands, and the wonder of that ebb and flow of life when the wildfowl whirl in at evening to the marshlands and at dawn pass out to sea. And she knew that over her head above the farmer's house stretched wide Paradise, where perhaps God was now imagining a sunrise while angels played low on lutes, and the sun came rising up on the world below to gladden fields and marsh.

And all that heaven thought, the marsh thought too; for the blue of the marsh was as the blue of heaven, and the great cloud shapes in heaven became the shapes in the marsh, and through each ran momentary rivers of purple, errant between banks of gold. And the stalwart army of reeds appeared out of the gloom with all their pennons waving as far as the eye could see. And from another window she saw the vast cathedral gathering its ponderous strength together, and lifting it up in towers out of the marshlands.

She said, "I will never, never leave the marsh."

An hour later she dressed with great difficulty and went down to eat the second meal of her life. The farmer and his wife were kindly folk, and taught her how to eat.

"I suppose the gypsies don't have knives and forks," one said to the other afterwards.

After breakfast the farmer went and saw the Dean, who lived near his cathedral, and presently returned and brought back to the Dean's house the little Wild Thing with the new soul.

"This is the lady," said the farmer. "This is Dean Murnith." Then he went away.

"Ah," said the Dean, "I understand you were lost the other night in the marshes. It was a terrible night to be lost in the marshes."

"I love the marshes," said the little Wild Thing with the new soul.

"Indeed! How old are you?" said the Dean.

"I don't know," she answered.

"You must know about how old you are," he said.

"Oh, about ninety," she said, "or more."

"Ninety years!" exclaimed the Dean.

"No, ninety centuries," she said; "I am as old as the marshes."

Then she told her story — how she had longed to be a human and go and worship God, and have a soul and see the beauty of the world, and how all the Wild Things had made her a soul of gossamer and mist and music and strange memories.

"But if this is true," said Dean Murnith, "this is very wrong. God cannot have intended you to have a soul."

"What is your name?"

"I have no name," she answered.

"We must find a Christian name and a surname for you. What would you like to be called?"

"Song of the Rushes," she said.

"That won't do at all," said the Dean.

"Then I would like to be called Terrible North Wind, or Star in the Waters," she said.

"No, no, no," said Dean Murnith; "that is quite impossible. We could call you Miss Rush if you like. How would Mary Rush do? Perhaps you had better have another name — say Mary Jane Rush."

So the little Wild Thing with the soul of the marshes took the names that were offered her, and became Mary Jane Rush.

"And we must find something for you to do," said Dean Murnith. "Meanwhile we can give you a room here."

"I don't want to do anything," replied Mary Jane; "I want to worship God in the cathedral and live beside the marshes."

Then Mrs. Murnith came in, and for the rest of that day Mary Jane stayed at the house of the Dean. And there with her new soul she perceived the beauty of the world; for it came grey and level out of misty distances, and widened into grassy fields and plow lands right up to the edge of an old gabled town; and solitary in the fields far off an ancient windmill stood, and his honest handmade sails went round and round in the free East Anglian winds. Close by, the gabled houses leaned out over the streets, planted fair upon sturdy timbers that grew in the olden time, all glorying among themselves upon their beauty. And out of them, buttress by buttress, growing and going upwards, aspiring tower by tower, rose the cathedral. And she saw the people moving in the streets all leisurely and slow, and unseen among them, whispering to each other, unheard by living men and concerned only with bygone things, drifted the ghosts of very long ago. And wherever the streets ran eastwards, wherever were gaps in the houses, always there broke into view the sight of the great marshes, like to some bar of music weird and strange that haunts a melody, arising again and again, played on the violin by one musician only, who plays no other bar, and he is swart and lank about the hair and bearded about the lips, and his moustache droops long and low, and no one knows the land from which he comes.

All these were good things for a new soul to see.

Then the sun set over green fields and plowland, and the night came up. One by one the merry lights of cheery lamp-lit windows took their stations in the solemn night.

Then the bells rang, far up in a cathedral tower, and their melody fell on the roofs of the old houses and poured over their eaves until the streets were full, and then flooded away over green fields and plow, till it came to the sturdy mill and brought the miller trudging to evensong, and far away eastwards and seawards the sound rang out over the remoter marshes. And it was all as yesterday to the old ghosts in the streets.

Then the Dean's wife took Mary Jane to evening service, and she saw three hundred candles filling all the aisle with light. But sturdy pillars stood there in unlit vastnesses; great colonnades going away into the gloom, where evening and morning, year in year out, they did their work in the dark, holding the cathedral roof aloft. And it was stiller than the marshes are still when the ice has come and the wind that brought it has fallen.

Suddenly into this stillness rushed the sound of the organ, roaring, and presently the people prayed and sang.

No longer could Mary Jane see their prayers ascending like thin gold chains, for that was but an elfin fancy, but she imagined clear in her new soul the seraphs passing in the ways of Paradise, and the angels changing guard to watch the World by night.

When the Dean had finished service, a young curate, Mr. Millings, went up into the pulpit.

He spoke of Abana and Pharpar, rivers of Damascus: and Mary Jane was glad that there were rivers having such names, and heard with wonder of Nineveh, that great city, and many things strange and new.

And the light of the candles shone on the curate's fair hair, and his voice went ringing down the aisle, and Mary Jane rejoiced that he was there. But when his voice stopped she felt a sudden loneliness. such as she had not felt since the making of the marshes; for the Wild Things never are lonely and never unhappy, but dance all night on the reflection of the stars, and, having no souls, desire nothing more.

After the collection was made, before anyone moved to go, Mary Jane walked up the aisle to Mr. Millings,

"I love you," she said.

# Chapter II

Nobody sympathized with Mary Jane. "So unfortunate for Mr. Millings," everyone said; "such a promising young man."

Mary Jane was sent away to a great manufacturing city of the Midlands, where work had been found for her in a cloth factory, And there was nothing in that town that was good for a soul to see. For it did not know that beauty was to be desired; so it made many things by machinery, and became hurried in all its ways, and boasted its superiority over other cities and

became richer and richer, and there was none to pity
it.

In this city Mary Jane had had lodgings found for
her near the factory.

At six o'clock on those November mornings, about
the time that, far away from the city, the wildfowl rose
up out of the calm marshes and passed to the troubled
spaces of the sea, at six o'clock the factory uttered a
prolonged howl and gathered the workers together, and
there they worked, saving two hours for food, the
whole of the daylit hours and into the dark till the
bells tolled six again.

There Mary Jane worked with other girls in a long
dreary room, where giants sat pounding wool into a
long threadlike strip with iron, rasping hands. And all
day long they roared as they sat at their soulless work.
But the work of Mary Jane was not with these, only
their roar was ever in her ears as their clattering iron
limbs went to and fro.

Her work was to tend a creature smaller, but infi-
nitely more cunning.

It took the strip of wool that the giants had threshed,
and whirled it round and round until it had twisted it
into hard thin thread. Then it would make a clutch
with fingers of steel at the thread that it had gathered,
and waddle away about five yards and come back with
more.

It had mastered all the subtlety of skilled workers,
and had gradually displaced them; one thing only it
could not do, it was unable to pick up the ends if a
piece of the thread broke, in order to tie them together
again. For this a human soul was required, and it was
Mary Jane's business to pick up broken ends; and the
moment she placed them together the busy soulless
creature tied them for itself.

All here was ugly; even the green wool as it whirled round and round was neither the green of the grass nor yet the green of the rushes, but a sorry muddy green that befitted a sullen city under a murky sky.

When she looked out over the roofs of the town, there too was ugliness; and well the houses knew it, for with hideous stucco they aped in grotesque mimicry the pillars and temples of old Greece, pretending to one another to be that I which they were not. And emerging from these houses and going in, and seeing the pretence of paint and stucco year after year until it all peeled away, the souls of the poor owners of those houses sought to be other souls until they grew weary of it.

At evening Mary Jane went back to her lodgings. Only then, after the dark had fallen, could the soul of Mary Jane perceive any beauty in that city, when the lamps were lit and here and there a star shone through the smoke. Then she would have gone abroad and beheld the night, but this the old woman to whom she was confided would not let her do. And the days multiplied themselves by seven and became weeks, and the weeks passed by, and all days were the same. And all the while the soul of Mary Jane was crying for beautiful things, and found not one, saving on Sundays, when she went to church, and left it to find the city greyer than before.

One day she decided that it was better to be a wild thing in the lovely marshes, than to have a soul that cried for beautiful things and found not one. From that day she determined to be rid of her soul, so she told her story to one of the factory girls, and said to her:

"The other girls are poorly clad and they do soulless work; surely some of them have no souls and would take mine."

But the factory girl said to her: "All the poor have souls. It is all they have."

Then Mary Jane watched the rich whenever she saw them, and vainly sought for someone without a soul.

One day at the hour when the machines rested and the human beings that tended them rested too, the wind being at that time from the direction of the marshlands, the soul of Mary Jane lamented bitterly. Then, as she stood outside the factory gates, the soul irresistibly compelled her to sing, and a wild song came from her lips, hymning the marshlands. And into her song came crying her yearning for home, and for the sound of the shout of the North Wind, masterful and proud, with his lovely lady the Snow; and she sang of tales that the rushes murmured to one another, tales that the teal knew and the watchful heron. And over the crowded streets her song went crying away, the song of waste places and of wild free lands, full of wonder and magic, for she had in her elf-made soul the song of the birds and the roar of the organ in the marshes.

At this moment Signor Thompsoni, the well-known English tenor, happened to go by with a friend. They stopped and listened; everyone stopped and listened.

"There has been nothing like this in Europe in my time," said Signor Thompsoni.

So a change came into the life of Mary Jane. People were written to, and finally it was arranged that she should take a leading part in the Covent Garden Opera in a few weeks.

So she went to London to learn. London and singing lessons were better than the City of the Midlands and those terrible machines. Yet still Mary Jane was not free to go and live as she liked by the edge of the marshlands, and she was still determined to be rid of her soul, but could find no one that had not a soul of their own.

One day she was told that the English people would not listen to her as Miss Rush, and was asked what more suitable name she would like to be called by.

"I would like to be called Terrible North Wind," said Mary Jane, "or Song of the Rushes."

When she was told that this was impossible and Signorina Maria Russiano was suggested, she acquiesced at once, as she had acquiesced when they took her away from her curate; she knew nothing of the ways of humans.

At last the day of the Opera came round, and it was a cold day of the winter.

And Signorina Russiano appeared on the stage before a crowded house.

And Signorina Russiano sang.

And into the song went all the longing of her soul, the soul that could not go to Paradise, but could only worship God and know the meaning of music, and the longing pervaded that Italian song as the infinite mystery of the hills is borne along the sound of distant sheep-bells. Then in the souls that were in that crowded house arose little memories of a great while since that were quite quite dead, and lived awhile again during that marvelous song.

And a strange chill went into the blood of all that listened, as though they stood on the border of bleak marshes and the North Wind blew.

And some it moved to sorrow and some to regret, and some to an unearthly joy — then suddenly the song went wailing away, like the winds of the winter from the marshlands when Spring appears from the South.

So it ended. And a great silence fell foglike over all that house, breaking in upon the end of a chatty conversation that Cecilia, Countess of Birmingham was enjoying with a friend.

In the dead hush Signorina Russiano rushed from the stage; she appeared again running among the audience, and dashed up to the lady.

"Take my soul," she said; "it is a beautiful soul. It can worship God, and knows the meaning of music and can imagine Paradise. And if you go to the marshlands with it you will see beautiful things; there is an old town there built of lovely timbers, with ghosts in its streets."

Lady Birmingham stared. Everyone was standing up. "See," said Signorina Russiano, "it is a beautiful soul."

And she clutched at her left breast a little above the heart, and there was the soul shining in her hand, with the green and blue lights going round and round and the purple flare in the midst,

"Take it," she said, "and you will love all that is beautiful, and know the four winds, each one by his name, and the songs of the birds at dawn. I do not want it, because I am not free. Put it to your left breast a little above the heart."

Still everybody was standing up, and Lady Birmingham felt uncomfortable.

"Please offer it to someone else," she said.

"But they all have souls already," said Signorina Russiano.

And everybody went on standing up. And Lady Birmingham took the soul in her hand.

"Perhaps it is lucky," she said.

She felt that she wanted to pray.

She half-closed her eyes, and said *"Unberufen."* Then she put the soul to her left breast a little above the heart, and hoped that the people would sit down and the singer go away.

Instantly a heap of clothes collapsed before her. For a moment, in the shadow among the seats, those who were born in the dusk hour might have seen a little brown thing leaping free from the clothes; then it sprang into the bright light of the hall, and became invisible to any human eye.

It dashed about for a little, then found the door, and presently was in the lamplit streets.

To those that were born in the dusk hour it might have been seen leaping rapidly wherever the streets ran northwards and eastwards, disappearing from human sight as it passed under the lamps, and appearing again beyond them with a marsh-light over its head.

Once a dog perceived it and gave chase, and was left far behind.

The cats of London, who are all born in the dusk hour, howled fearfully as it went by.

Presently it came to the meaner streets, where the houses are smaller. Then it went due northeastwards, leaping from roof to roof. And so in a few minutes it came to more open spaces, and then to the desolate lands, where market gardens grow, which are neither town nor country. Till at last the good black trees came into view, with their demoniac shapes in the night, and the grass was cold and wet, and the night-mist floated over it. And a great white owl came by, going up and down in the dark. And at all these things the little Wild Thing rejoiced elvishly.

And it left London far behind it, reddening the sky, and could distinguish no longer its unlovely roar, but heard again the noises of the night.

And now it would come through a hamlet glowing and comfortable in the night; and now to the dark, wet, open fields again; and many an owl it overtook as they drifted through the night, a people friendly to the Elf-folk. Sometimes it crossed wide rivers, leaping from star to star; and, choosing its way as it went, to avoid the hard rough roads, came before midnight to the East Anglian lands. And it heard there the shout of the

North Wind, who was dominant and angry, as he drove southwards his adventurous geese; while the rushes bent before him chaunting plaintively and low, like enslaved rowers of some fabulous trireme, bending and swinging under blows of the lash, and singing all the while a doleful song.

And it felt the good dank air that clothes by night the broad East Anglian lands, and came again to some old perilous pool where the soft green mosses grew, and there plunged downward and downward into the dear dark water, till it felt the homely ooze once more coming up between its toes. Thence, out of the lovely chill that is in the heart of the ooze, it arose renewed and rejoicing to dance upon the image of the stars.

I chanced to stand that night by the marsh's edge, forgetting in my mind the affairs of men; and I saw the marshfires come leaping up from all the perilous places. And they came up by flocks the whole night long to the number of a great multitude, and danced away together over the marshes. And I believe that there was a great rejoicing all that night among the kith of the Elffolk.

# The Highwayman

*T*om o' the Roads had ridden his last ride, and was now alone in the night. From where he was, a man might see the white recumbent sheep and the black outline of the lonely downs, and the grey line of the farther and lonelier downs beyond them; or in hollows far below him, out of the pitiless wind, he might see the grey smoke of hamlets arising from black valleys. But all alike was black to the eyes of Tom, and all the sounds were silence in his ears; only his soul struggled to slip from the iron chains and to pass southwards into Paradise. And the wind blew and blew.

For Tom tonight had naught but the wind to ride; they had taken his true black horse on the day when they took from him the green fields and the sky, men's voices and the laughter of women, and had left him alone with chains about his neck to swing in the wind forever. And the wind blew and blew.

But the soul of Tom o' the Roads was nipped by cruel chains, and whenever it struggled to escape it was beaten backwards into the iron collar by the wind that blows from Paradise from the south. And swinging there by the neck, there fell away old sneers from off his lips, and scoffs that he had long since scoffed at God fell from his tongue, and there rotted old bad lusts out of his heart, and from his fingers the stains of deeds that were evil; and they all fell to the ground and grew there in pallid rings and clusters. And when these ill things had all fallen away, Tom's soul was clean again, as his early love had found it, a long while since in spring; and it swung up there in the wind with the bones of Tom, and with his old torn coat and rusty chains.

And the wind blew and blew.

And ever and anon the souls of the sepulchered, coming from consecrated acres, would go by beating up wind to Paradise past the Gallows Tree and past the soul of Tom, that might not go free.

Night after night Tom watched the sheep upon the downs with empty hollow sockets, till his dead hair grew and covered his poor dead face, and hid the shame of it from the sheep. And the wind blew and blew.

Sometimes on gusts of the wind came someone's tears, and beat and beat again against the iron chains, but could not rust them through. And the wind blew and blew.

And every evening all the thoughts that Tom had ever uttered came flocking in from doing their work in the world, the work that may not cease, and sat along the gallows branches and chirruped to the soul of Tom, the soul that might not go free. All the thoughts that he had ever uttered! And the evil thoughts rebuked the soul that bore them because they might not die. And all those that he had uttered the most furtively, chirruped the loudest and the shrillest in the branches all the night.

And all the thoughts that Tom had ever thought about himself now pointed at the wet bones and mocked at the old torn coat. But the thoughts that he had of others were the only companions that his soul had to soothe it in the night as it swung to and fro. And they twittered to the soul and cheered the poor dumb thing that could have dreams no more, till there came a murderous thought and drove them all away.

And the wind blew and blew.

Paul, Archbishop of Alois and Vayence, lay in his white sepulcher of marble, facing full to the south-wards towards Paradise. And over his tomb was sculptured the Cross of Christ, that his soul might have repose. No wind howled here as it howled in lonely tree-tops up upon the downs, but came with gentle breezes, orchard scented, over the low lands from Paradise from the southwards, and played about forget-me-nots and grasses in the consecrated land where lay the Reposeful round the sepulcher of Paul, Archbishop of Alois and Vayence. Easy it was for a man's soul to pass from such a sepulcher, and, flitting low over remembered fields, to come upon the garden lands of Paradise and find eternal ease.

And the wind blew and blew.

In a tavern of foul repute three men were lapping gin. Their names were Joe and Will and the gypsy Puglioni; no other names had they, for of whom their fathers were they had no knowledge, but only dark suspicions.

Sin had caressed and stroked their faces often with its paws, but the face of Puglioni Sin had kissed all over the mouth and chin. Their food was robbery and their pastime murder. All of them had incurred the sorrow of God and the enmity of man. They sat at a table with a pack of cards before them, all greasy with the marks of cheating thumbs. And they whispered to one another over their gin, but so low that the landlord of the tavern at the other end of the room could hear only muffled oaths, and knew not by Whom they swore or what they said.

These three were the staunchest friends that ever God had given unto a man. And he to whom their friendship had been given had nothing else besides, saving some bones that swung in the wind and rain, and an old torn coat and iron chains, and a soul that might not go free.

But as the night wore on the three friends left their gin and stole away, and crept down to that graveyard where rested in his sepulcher Paul, Archbishop of Alois and Vayence. At the edge of the graveyard, but outside the consecrated ground, they dug a hasty grave, two digging while one watched in the wind and the rain. And the worms that crept in the unhallowed ground wondered and waited.

And the terrible hour of midnight came upon them with its fears, and found them still beside the place of tombs. And the three friends trembled at the horror of such an hour in such a place, and shivered in the wind and drenching rain, but still worked on. And the wind blew and blew.

Soon they had finished. And at once they left the hungry grave with all its worms unfed, and went away over the wet fields stealthily but in haste, leaving the place of tombs behind them in the midnight. And as they went they shivered, and each man as he shivered cursed the rain aloud. And so they came to the spot where they had hidden a ladder and a lantern. There they held long debate whether they should light the lantern, or whether they should go without it for fear of the King's men. But in the end it seemed to them better that they should have the light of their lantern, and risk being taken by the King's men and hanged, than that they should come suddenly face to face in the darkness with whatever one might come face to face with a little after midnight about the Gallows Tree.

On three roads in England whereon it was not the wont of folk to go their ways in safety, travelers tonight went unmolested. But the three friends, walking several paces wide of the King's highway, approached the Gallows Tree, and Will carried the lantern and Joe the ladder, but Puglioni carried a great sword wherewith to do the work which must be done. When they came close, they saw how bad was the case with Tom, for little remained of that fine figure of a man and nothing at all of his great resolute spirit, only as they came they thought they heard a whimpering cry like the sound of a thing that was caged and unfree.

To and fro, to and fro in the winds swung the bones and the soul of Tom, for the sins that he had sinned on the King's highway against the laws of the King; and with shadows and a lantern through the darkness, at the peril of their lives, came the three friends that his soul had won before it swung in chains. Thus the seeds of Tom's own soul that he had sown all his life had grown into a Gallows Tree that bore in season iron chains in clusters; while the careless seeds that he had strewn here and there, a kindly jest and a few merry words, had grown into the triple friendship that would not desert his bones.

Then the three set the ladder against the tree, and Puglioni went up with his sword in his right hand, and at the top of it he reached up and began to hack at the neck below the iron collar. Presently, the bones and the old coat and the soul of Tom fell down with a rattle, and a moment afterwards his head that had watched so long alone swung clear from the swinging chain. These things Will and Joe gathered up, and Puglioni came running down his ladder, and they heaped upon its rungs the terrible remains of their friend, and has-

tened away wet through with the rain, with the fear of
phantoms in their hearts and horror lying before them
on the ladder. By two o'clock they were down again in
the valley out of the bitter wind, but they went on past
the open grave into the graveyard all among the tombs,
with their lantern and their ladder and the terrible
thing upon it, which kept their friendship still. Then
these three, that had robbed the Law of its due and
proper victim, still sinned on for what was still their
friend, and levered out the marble slabs from the sacred
sepulcher of Paul, Archbishop of Alois and Vayence.
And from it they took the very bones of the Archbishop himself, and carried them away to the eager
grave that they had left, and put them in and shoveled
back the earth. But all that lay on the ladder they
placed, with a few tears, within the great white sepulcher under the Cross of Christ, and put back the
marble slabs.

Thence the soul of Tom, arising hallowed out of
sacred ground, went at dawn down the valley, and,
lingering a little about his mother's cottage and old
haunts of childhood, passed on and came to the wide
lands beyond the clustered homesteads. There, there
met with it all the kindly thoughts that the soul of Tom
had ever had, and they flew and sang beside it all the
way southwards, until at last, with singing all about it,
it came to Paradise.

But Will and Joe and the gypsy Puglioni went back
to their gin, and robbed and cheated again in the tavern
of foul repute, and knew not that in their sinful lives
they had sinned one sin at which the Angels smiled.

# In the Twilight

The lock was quite crowded with boats when we capsized. I went down backwards for some few feet before I started to swim, then I came spluttering upwards towards the light; but, instead of reaching the surface, I hit my head against the keel of a boat and went down again. I struck out almost at once and came up, but before I reached the surface my head crashed against a boat for the second time, and I went right to the bottom. I was confused and thoroughly frightened. I was desperately in need of air, and knew that if I hit a boat for the third time I should never see the surface again. Drowning is a horrible death, notwithstanding all that has been said to the contrary. My past life never occurred to my mind, but I thought of many trivial things that I might not do or see again if I were drowned. I swam up in a slanting direction, hoping to avoid the boat that I had struck. Suddenly I saw all the boats in the lock quite clearly just above me, and every one of their curved varnished planks and the scratches and chips upon their keels. I saw several gaps among the boats where I might have swam up to the surface, but it did not seem worthwhile to try and get there, and I had forgotten why I wanted to. Then all the people leaned over the sides of their boats: I saw the light flannel suits of the men and the colored flowers in the women's hats, and I noticed details of their dresses quite distinctly. Everybody in the boats was looking down at me; then they all said to one another, "We must leave him now," and they and the boats went away; and there was nothing above me but the river and the sky, and on either side of me were the green weeds that grew in the mud, for I had somehow sunk back to the bottom again. The river as it flowed by murmured not unpleasantly in my ears, and the rushes seemed to be whispering quite softly among themselves. Presently the murmuring of the river took the form of words, and I heard it say, "We must go on to the sea; we must leave him now."

Then the river went away, and both its banks; and the rushes whispered, "Yes, we must leave him now." And they, too, departed, and I was left in a great emptiness staring up at the blue sky. Then the great sky bent over me, and spoke quite softly like a kindly nurse soothing some little foolish child, and the sky said, "Good-bye. All will be well. Good-bye." And I was sorry to lose the blue sky, but the sky went away. Then I was alone, with nothing roundabout me; I could see no light, but it was not dark — there was just absolutely nothing, above me and below me and on every side. I thought that perhaps I was dead, and that this might be eternity; when suddenly some great southern hills rose up all round about me, and I was lying on I the warm grassy slope of a valley in England. It was a valley that I had known well when I was young, but I had not seen it now for many years. Beside me stood the tall flower of the mint; I saw the sweet-smelling thyme flower and one or two wild strawberries. There came up to me from fields below me the beautiful smell of hay, and there was a break in the voice of the cuckoo. There was a feeling of summer and of evening and of lateness and of Sabbath in the air; the sky was calm and full of a strange color, and the sun was low; the bells in the church in the village were all a-ring, and the chimes went wandering with echoes up the valley towards the sun, and whenever the echoes died a new chime was born. And all the people of the village walked up a stone-paved path under a black oak porch and went into the church, and the chimes stopped and the people of the village began to sing, and the level sunlight shone on the white tombstones that stood all round the church. Then there was a stillness in the village, and shouts and laughter came up from the valley no more, only the occasional sound of the organ and of song. And the blue butterflies, those that love the chalk, came and perched themselves on the tall grasses, five or six sometimes on a single piece of grass, and they closed their wings and slept, and the grass bent a little beneath them. And from the woods along the tops of the hills the rabbits came hopping out and nibbled the grass, and hopped a little further and nibbled again, and the large daisies closed their petals up and the birds began to sing.

Then the hills spoke, all the great chalk hills that I loved, and with a deep and solemn voice they said, "We have come to you to say Good-bye."

Then they all went away, and there was nothing again all round about me upon every side. I looked everywhere for something on which to rest the eye. Nothing. Suddenly a low grey sky swept over me and a moist air met my face; a great plain rushed up to me from the edge of the clouds; on two sides it touched the sky, and on two sides between it and the clouds a line of low hills lay. One line of hills brooded grey in the distance, the other stood a patchwork of little square green fields, with a few white cottages about it. The plain was an archipelago of a million islands each about a yard square or less, and everyone of them was red with heather. I was back on the Bog of Allen again after many years, and it was just the same as ever, though I had heard that they were draining it. I was with an old friend whom I was glad to see again, for they had told me that he died some years ago. He seemed strangely young, but what surprised me most was that he stood upon a piece of bright green moss which I had always learned to think would never bear. I was glad, too, to see the old bog again, and all the lovely things that grew there — the scarlet mosses and the green mosses and the firm and friendly heather, and the deep silent water. I saw a little stream that wandered vaguely through the bog, and little white shells down in the clear depths of it; I saw, a little way off, one of the great pools where no islands are, with rushes round its borders, where the ducks love to come. I looked long at that untroubled world of heather, and then I looked at the white cottages on the hill, and saw the grey smoke curling from their chimneys and knew that they burned turf there, and longed for the smell of burning turf again. And far away there arose and came nearer the weird cry of wild and happy voices, and a flock of geese appeared that was coming from the northward. Then their cries blended into one great voice of exultation, the voice of freedom, the voice of Ireland, the voice of the Waste; and the voice said "Good-bye to you. Good-bye!" and passed away into the distance; and as it passed, the tame geese on the farms cried out to their brothers up above them that they were free. Then the hills went away, and the bog and the sky went with them, and I was alone again, as lost souls are alone.

Then there grew up beside me the red brick buildings of my first school and the chapel that adjoined it. The fields a little way off were full of boys in white flannels playing cricket. On the asphalt playing ground, just by the schoolroom windows, stood Agamemnon, Achilles, and Odysseus, with their Argives armed behind them; but Hector stepped down out of a ground-floor window, and in the schoolroom were all Priam's sons and the Achæans and fair Helen; and a little farther away the Ten Thousand drifted across the playground, going up into the heart of Persia to place Cyrus on his brother's throne. And the boys that I knew called to me from the fields, and said "Good-bye," and they and the fields went away; and the Ten Thousand said "Good-bye," each file as they passed me marching swiftly, and they too disappeared. And Hector and Agamemnon said "Good-bye," and the host of the Argives and of the Achæans; and they all went away and the old school with them, and I was alone again.

The next scene that filled the emptiness was rather dim: I was being led by my nurse along a little footpath over a common in Surrey. She was quite young. Close by a band of gypsies had lit their fire, near them their romantic caravan stood unhorsed, and the horse cropped grass beside it. It was evening, and the gypsies muttered round their fire in a tongue unknown and strange. Then they all said in English, "Good-bye." And the evening and the common and the campfire went away. And instead of this a white highway with darkness and stars below it that led into darkness and stars, but at the near end of the road were common fields and gardens, and there I stood close to a large number of people, men and women. And I saw a man walking alone down the road away from me towards the darkness and the stars, and all the people called him by his name, and the man would not hear them, but walked on down the road, and the people went on calling him by his name. But I became irritated with the man because he would not stop or turn round when so many people called him by his name, and it was a very strange name. And I became weary of hearing the strange name so very often repeated, so that I made a great effort to call him, that he might listen and that the people might stop repeating this strange name. And with the effort I opened my eyes wide, and the name that the people called was my own name, and I lay on the river's bank with men and women bending over me, and my hair was wet.

# The Ghosts

$T$he argument that I had with my brother in his great lonely house will scarcely interest my readers. Not those, at least, whom I hope may be attracted by the experiment that I undertook, and by the strange things that befell me in that hazardous region into which so lightly and so ignorantly I allowed my fancy to enter. It was at Oneleigh that I had visited him.

Now Oneleigh stands in a wide isolation, in the midst of a dark gathering of old whispering cedars. They nod their heads together when the North Wind comes, and nod again and agree, and furtively grow still again, and say no more awhile. The North Wind is to them like a nice problem among wise old men; they nod their heads over it, and mutter about it all together. They know much, those cedars, they have been there so long. Their grandsires knew Lebanon, and the grandsires of these were the servants of the King of Tyre and came to Solomon's court. And amidst these black-haired children of grey-headed Time stood the old house of Oneleigh. I know not how many centuries had lashed against it their evanescent foam of years; but it was still unshattered, and all about it

were the things of long ago, as cling strange growths
to some seadefying rock. Here, like the shells of long-
dead limpets, was armor that men encased themselves
in long ago; here, too, were tapestries of many colors,
beautiful as seaweed; no modern flotsam ever drifted
hither, no early Victorian furniture, no electric light.
The great trade routes that littered the years with empty
meat tins and cheap novels were far from here. Well,
well, the centuries will shatter it and drive its fragments
on to distant shores. Meanwhile, while it yet stood, I
went on a visit there to my brother, and we argued
about ghosts. My brother's intelligence on this subject
seemed to me to be in need of correction. He mistook
things imagined for things having an actual existence;
he argued that second-hand evidence of persons having
seen ghosts proved ghosts to exist. I said that even if
they had seen ghosts, this was no proof at all; nobody
believes that there are red rats, though there is plenty
of first-hand evidence of men having seen them in
delirium. Finally, I said I would see ghosts myself, and
continue to argue against their actual existence. So I
collected a handful of cigars and drank several cups of
very strong tea, and went without my dinner, and
retired into a room where there was dark oak and all
the chairs were covered with tapestry; and my brother
went to bed bored with our argument, and trying hard
to dissuade me from making myself uncomfortable.
All the way up the old stairs as I stood at the bottom
of them, and as his candle went winding up and up, I
heard him still trying to persuade me to have supper
and go to bed.

It was a windy winter, and outside the cedars were
muttering I know not what about; but I think that they
were Tories of a school long dead, and were troubled
about something new. Within, a great damp log upon
the fireplace began to squeak and sing, and struck up

a whining tune, and a tall flame stood up over it and
beat time, and all the shadows crowded round and
began to dance. In distant corners old masses of darkness sat still like chaperones and never moved. Over
there, in the darkest part of the room, stood a door
that was always locked. It led into the hall, but no one
ever used it; near that door something had happened
once of which the family are not proud. We do not
speak of it. There in the firelight stood the venerable
forms of the old chairs; the hands that had made their
tapestries lay far beneath the soil, the needles with
which they wrought were many separate flakes of rust.
No one wove now in that old room — no one but the
assiduous ancient spiders who, watching by the death-
bed of things of yore, worked shrouds to hold their
dust. In shrouds about the cornices already lay the
heart of the oak wainscot that the worm had eaten out.

Surely at such an hour, in such a room, a fancy
already excited by hunger and strong tea might see the
ghosts of former occupants. I expected nothing less.
The fire flickered and the shadows danced, memories
of strange historic things rose vividly in my mind; but
midnight chimed solemnly from a seven-foot clock,
and nothing happened. My imagination would not be
hurried, and the chill that is with the small hours had
come upon me, and I had nearly abandoned myself to
sleep, when in the hall adjoining there arose the
rustling of silk dresses that I had waited for and expected. Then there entered two by two the highborn
ladies and their gallants of Jacobean times. They were
little more than shadows — very dignified shadows, and
almost indistinct; but you have all read ghost stories
before, you have all seen in museums the dresses of
those times — there is little need to describe them; they
entered, several of them, and sat down on the old
chairs, perhaps a little carelessly considering the value

of the tapestries. Then the rustling of their dresses ceased.

Well — I had seen ghosts, and was neither frightened nor convinced that ghosts existed. I was about to get up out of my chair and go to bed, when there came a sound of pattering in the hall, a sound of bare feet coming over the polished floor, and every now and then a foot would slip and I heard claws scratching along the wood as some four-footed thing lost and regained its balance. I was not frightened, but uneasy. The pattering came straight towards the room that I was in, then I heard the sniffing of expectant nostrils; perhaps "uneasy" was not the most suitable word to describe my feelings then. Suddenly a herd of black creatures larger than bloodhounds came galloping in; they had large pendulous ears, their noses were to the ground sniffing, they went up to the lords and ladies of long ago and fawned about them disgustingly. Their eyes were horribly bright, and ran down to great depths. When I looked into them I knew suddenly what these creatures were, and I was afraid. They were the sins, the filthy, immortal sins of those courtly men and women.

How demure she was, the lady that sat near me on an old-world chair — how demure she was, and how fair, to have beside her with its jowl upon her lap a sin with such cavernous red eyes, a clear case of murder. And you, yonder lady with the golden hair, surely not you — and yet that fearful beast with the yellow eyes slinks from you to yonder courtier there, and whenever one drives it away it slinks back to the other. Over there a lady tries to smile as she strokes the loathsome furry head of another's sin, but one of her own is jealous and intrudes itself under her hand. Here sits an old nobleman with his grandson on his knee, and one of the great black sins of the grandfather is licking the child's face and has made the child its own. Sometimes a ghost would move and seek another chair, but always his pack of sins would move behind him. Poor ghosts, poor ghosts! how many flights they must have attempted for two hundred years from their hated sins, how many excuses they must have given for their presence, and the sins were with them still — and still unexplained. Suddenly one of them seemed to scent my living blood, and bayed horribly, and all the others left their ghosts at once and dashed up to the sin that had given tongue. The brute had picked up my scent near the door by which I had entered, and they moved slowly nearer to me sniffing along the floor, and uttering every now and then their fearful cry. I saw that the whole thing had gone too far. But now they had seen me, now they were all about me, they sprang up trying to reach my throat; and whenever their claws touched me, horrible thoughts came into my mind and unutterable desires dominated my heart. I planned bestial things as these creatures leaped around me, and planned them with a masterly cunning. A great red-eyed murder was among the foremost of those furry things from whom I feebly strove to defend my throat. Suddenly it seemed to me good that I should kill my brother. It seemed important to me that I should not risk being punished. I knew where a revolver was kept; after I had shot him, I would dress the body up and put flour on the face like a man that had been acting as a ghost. It would be very simple. I would say that he had frightened me — and the servants had heard us talking about ghosts. There were one or two trivialities that would have to be arranged, but nothing escaped my mind. Yes, it seemed to me very good that I should kill my brother as I looked into the red depths of this creature's eyes. But one last effort as they dragged me down — "If two straight lines cut one another," I said, "the opposite angles are equal. Let AB, CD, cut one another at E, then the angles CEA, CEB equal two right angles (prop. xiii.). Also CEA, AED equal two right angles."

I moved towards the door to get the revolver; a hideous exultation arose among the beasts. "But the angle CEA is common, therefore AED equals CEB. In the same way CEA equals DEB. Q.E.D." It was proved. Logic and reason reestablished themselves in my mind, there were no dark hounds of sin, the tapestried chairs were empty. It seemed to me an inconceivable thought that a man should murder his brother.

# The Whirlpool

Once going down to the shore of the great sea I came upon the Whirlpool lying prone upon the sand and stretching his huge limbs in the sun.

I said to him: "Who art thou?"

And he said:

"I am named Nooz Wana, the Whelmer of Ships, and from the Straits of Pondar abed I am come, wherein it is my wont to vex the seas. There I chased Leviathan with my hands when he was young and strong; often he slipped through my fingers, and away into the weed forests that grow below the storms in the dusk on the floor of the sea; but at last I caught and tamed him. For there I lurk upon the ocean's floor, midway between the knees of either cliff, to guard the passage of the Straits from all the ships that seek the Further Seas; and whenever the white sails of the tall ships come swelling round the comer of the crag out of the sunlit spaces of the Known Sea and into the dark of the Straits, then standing firm upon the ocean's floor, with my knees a little bent, I take the waters of the Straits in both my hands and whirl them round my head. But the ship comes gliding on with the sound of the sailors singing on her decks, all singing songs of the islands and carrying the rumor of their cities to the lonely seas, till they see me suddenly astride athwart their course, and are caught in the waters as I whirl them round my head. Then I draw in the waters of the Straits towards me and downwards, nearer and nearer to my terrible feet, and hear in my ears above the roar of my waters the ultimate cry of the ship; for just before I drag them to the floor of ocean and stamp them asunder with my wrecking feet, ships utter their ultimate cry, and with it go the lives of all the sailors and passes the soul of the ship. And in the ultimate cry of ships are the songs the sailors sing, and their hopes and all their loves, and the song of the wind among the masts and timbers when they stood in the forest long ago, and the whisper of the rain that made them grow, and the soul of the tall pine tree or the oak. All this a ship gives up in one cry which she makes at the last. And at that moment I would pity the tall ship if I might; but a man may feel pity who sits in comfort by his fireside telling tales in the winter — no pity are they permitted ever to feel who do the work of the gods; and so when I have brought her circling from round my shoulders to my waist and thence, with her masts all sloping inwards, to my knees, and lower still and downwards till her topmast pennants flutter against my ankles, then I, Nooz Wana, Whelmer of Ships, lift up my feet and trample her beams asunder, and there go up again to the surface of the Straits only a few broken, timbers and the memories of the sailors and of their early loves to drift forever down the empty seas.

"Once in every hundred years, for one day only, I go to rest myself along the shore and to sun my limbs on the sand, that the tall ships may go through the unguarded Straits and find the Happy Isles. And the

Happy Isles stand midmost among the smiles of the sunny Further Seas, and there the sailors may come upon content and long for nothing; or if they long for aught, they shall possess it.

"There comes not Time with his devouring hours; nor any of the evils of the gods or men. These are the islands whereto the souls of the sailors every night put in from all the world to rest from going up and down the seas, to behold again the vision of far-off intimate hills that lift their orchards high above the fields facing the sunlight, and for a while again to speak with the souls of old. But about the dawn dreams twitter and arise, and circling thrice around the Happy Isles set out again to find the world of men, then follow the souls of the sailors, as, at evening, with slow stroke of stately wings the heron follows behind the flight of multitudinous rooks; but the souls returning find awakening bodies and endure the toil of the day. Such are the Happy Isles, whereunto few have come, save but as roaming shadows in the night, and for only a little while.

"But longer than is needed to make me strong and fierce again I may not stay, and at set of sun, when my arms are strong again and when I feel in my legs that I can plant them fair and bent upon the floor of ocean, then I go back to take a new grip upon the waters of the Straits, and to guard the Further Seas again for a hundred years. Because the gods are jealous, lest too many men shall pass to the Happy Isles and find content. *For the gods have not content.*"

# The Hurricane

One night I sat alone on the great down, looking over the edge of it at a murky, sullen city. All day long with its smoke it had troubled the holy sky, and now it sat there roaring in the distance and glared at me with its furnaces and lighted factory windows. Suddenly I became aware that I was not the only enemy of that city, for I perceived the colossal form of the Hurricane walking over the down towards me, playing idly with the flowers as he passed, and near me he stopped and spake to the Earthquake, who had come up molelike but vast out of a cleft in the earth.

"Old friend," said the Hurricane, "rememberest when we wrecked the nations and drave the herds of the sea into new pasturage?"

"Yes," said the Earthquake, drowsily; "Yes, yes."

"Old friend," said the Hurricane, "there are cities everywhere. Over thy head while thou didst sleep they have built them constantly. My four children the Winds suffocate with the fumes of them, the valleys are desolate of flowers, and the lovely forests are cut down since last we went abroad together."

The Earthquake lay there, with his snout towards the city, blinking at the lights, while the tall Hurricane stood beside him pointing fiercely at it.

"Come," said the Hurricane, "let us fare forth again and destroy them, that all the lovely forests may come back and the furry creeping things. Thou shalt whelm these cities utterly and drive the people forth, and I will smite them in the shelterless places and sweep their desecrations from the sea. Wilt thou come forth with me and do this thing for the glory of it? Wilt thou wreck the world again as we did, thou and I, or ever Man had come? Wilt thou come forth to this place at this hour tomorrow night?"

"Yes," said the Earthquake, "Yes," and he crept to his cleft again, and head foremost waddled down into the abysses.

When the Hurricane strode away, I got up quietly and departed, but at that hour of the next night I came up cautiously to the same spot. There I found the huge grey form of the Hurricane alone, with his head bowed in his hands, weeping; for the Earthquake sleeps long and heavily in the abysses, and he would not wake.

# The Fortress Unvanquishable,
# Save for Sacnoth

*I*n a wood older than record, a foster brother of the hills, stood the village of Allathurion; and there was peace between the people of that village and all the folk who walked in the dark ways of the wood, whether they were human or of the tribes of the beasts or of the race of the fairies and the elves and the little sacred spirits of trees and streams. Moreover, the village people had peace among themselves and between them and their lord, Lorendiac. In front of the village was a wide and grassy space, and beyond this the great wood again, but at the back the trees came right up to the houses, which, with their great beams and wooden framework and thatched roofs, green with moss, seemed almost to be a part of the forest.

Now in the time I tell of, there was trouble in Allathurion, for of an evening fell dreams were wont to come slipping through the tree trunks and into the peaceful village; and they assumed dominion of men's minds and led them in watches of the night through the cindery plains of Hell. Then the magician of that village made spells against those fell dreams; yet still the dreams came flitting through the trees as soon as the dark had fallen, and led men's minds by night into terrible places and caused them to praise Satan openly with their lips.

And men grew afraid of sleep in Allathurion. And they grew worn and pale, some through the want of rest, and others from fear of the things they saw on the cindery plains of Hell.

Then the magician of the village went up into the tower of his house, and all night long those whom fear kept awake could see his window high up in the night glowing softly alone. The next day, when the twilight was far gone and night was gathering fast, the magician went away to the forest's edge, and uttered there the spell that he had made. And the spell was a compulsive, terrible thing, having a power over evil dreams and over spirits of ill; for it was a verse of forty lines in many languages, both living and dead, and had in it the word wherewith the people of the plains are wont to curse their camels, and the shout wherewith the whalers of the north lure the whales shoreward to be killed, and a word that causes elephants to trumpet; and every one of the forty lines closed with a rhyme for "wasp."

And still the dreams came flitting through the forest, and led men's souls into the plains of Hell. Then the magician knew that the dreams were from Gaznak. Therefore he gathered the people of the village, and told them that he had uttered his mightiest spell — -a spell having power over all that were human or of the tribes of the beasts; and that since it had not availed the dreams must come from Gaznak, the greatest magician among the spaces of the stars. And he read to the people out of the Book of Magicians, which tells the comings of the comet and foretells his coming again. And he told them how Gaznak rides upon the comet, and how he visits Earth once in every two hundred and thirty years, and makes for himself a vast, invincible fortress and sends out dreams to feed on the minds of men, and may never be vanquished but by the sword Sacnoth.

And a cold fear fell on the hearts of the villagers when they found that their magician had failed them.

Then spake Leothric, son of the Lord Lorendiac, and twenty years old was he: "Good Master, what of the sword Sacnoth?"

And the village magician answered: "Fair Lord, no such sword as yet is wrought, for it lies as yet in the hide of Tharagavverug, protecting his spine."

Then said Leothric: "Who is Tharagavverug, and where may he be encountered?"

And the magician of Allathurion answered: "He is the dragon-crocodile who haunts the Northern marshes and ravages the homesteads by their marge. And the hide of his back is of steel, and his under parts are of iron; but along the midst of his back, over his spine, there lies a narrow strip of unearthly steel. This strip of steel is Sacnoth, and it may be neither cleft nor molten, and there is nothing in the world that may avail to break it, nor even leave a scratch upon its surface. It is of the length of a good sword, and of the breadth thereof. Shouldst thou prevail against Thara-gavverug, his hide may be melted away from Sacnoth in a furnace; but there is only one thing that may sharpen Sacnoth's edge, and this is one of Tharagav-verug's own steel eyes; and the other eye thou must fasten to Sacnoth's hilt, and it will watch for thee. But it is a hard task to vanquish Tharagavverug, for no sword can pierce his hide; his back cannot be broken, and he can neither burn nor drown. In one way only can Tharagavverug die, and that is by starving."

Then sorrow fell upon Leothric, but the magician spoke on:

"If a man drive Tharagavverug away from his food with a stick for three days, he will starve on the third day at sunset. And though he is not vulnerable, yet in one spot he may take hurt, for his nose is only of lead. A sword would merely lay bare the uncleavable bronze beneath, but if his nose be smitten constantly with a stick he will always recoil from the pain, and thus may Tharagavverug, to left and right, be driven away from his food."

Then Leothric said: "What is Tharagavverug's food?"

And the magician of Allathurion said: "His food is men."

But Leothric went straightway thence, and cut a great staff from a hazel tree, and slept early that evening. But the next morning, awaking from troubled dreams, he arose before the dawn, and, taking with him provisions for five days, set out through the forest northwards towards the marshes. For some hours he moved through the gloom of the forest, and when he emerged from it the sun was above the horizon shining on pools of water in the waste land. Presently he saw the claw-marks of Tharagavverug deep in the soil, and the track of his tail between them like a furrow in a field. Then Leothric followed the tracks till he heard the bronze heart of Tharagavverug before him, booming like a bell.

And Tharagavverug, it being the hour when he took the first meal of the day, was moving towards a village with his heart tolling. And all the people of the village were come out to meet him, is it was their wont to do; for they abode not the suspense of awaiting Tharagav-verug and of hearing him sniffing brazenly as he went

from door to door, pondering slowly in his metal mind
what habitant he should choose. And none dared to
flee, for in the days when the villagers fled from Tharagavverug, he, having chosen his victim, would track
him tirelessly, like a doom. Nothing availed them
against Tharagavverug. Once they climbed the trees
when he came, but Tharagavverug went up to one,
arching his back and leaning over slightly, and rasped
against the trunk until it fell. And when Leothric came
near, Tharagavverug saw him out of one of his small
steel eyes and came towards him leisurely, and the
echoes of his heart swirled up through his open mouth.
And Leothric stepped sideways from his onset, and
came between him and the village and smote him on
the nose, and the blow of the stick made a dint in the
soft lead. And Tharagavverug swung clumsily away,
uttering one fearful cry like the sound of a great church
bell that had become possessed of a soul that fluttered
upward from the tombs at night — -an evil soul, giving
the bell a voice. Then he attacked Leothric, snarling,
and again Leothric leapt aside, and smote him on the
nose with his stick. Tharagavverug sounded like a bell
howling. And whenever the dragon-crocodile attacked
him, or turned towards the village, Leothric smote him
again.

So all day long Leothric drove the monster with a
stick and he drove him further and further from his
prey, with his heart tolling angrily and his voice crying
out for pain.

Towards evening Tharagavverug ceased to snap at
Leothric, but ran before him to avoid the stick, for his
nose was sore and shining; and in the gloaming the
villagers came out and danced to cymbal and psaltery.
When Tharagavverug heard the cymbal and psaltery,
hunger and anger came upon him, and he felt as some
lord might feel who was held by force from the banquet

in his own castle and heard the creaking spit go round
and round and the good meat crackling on it. And all
that night he attacked Leothric fiercely, and oft-times
nearly caught him in the darkness; for his gleaming
eyes of steel could see as well by night as by day. And
Leothric gave ground slowly till the dawn, and when
the light came they were near the village again; yet not
so near to it as they had been when they encountered,
for Leothric drove Tharagavverug further in the day
than Tharagavverug had forced him back in the night.
Then Leothric drove him again with his stick till the
hour came when it was the custom of the dragon-crocodile to find his man. One third of his man he would
eat at the time he found him, and the rest at noon and
evening. But when the hour came for finding his man
a great fierceness came on Tharagavverug, and he
grabbed rapidly at Leothric, but could not seize him,
and for a long while neither of them would retire. But
at last the pain of the stick on his leaden nose overcame
the hunger of the dragon — crocodile, and he turned
from it howling. From that moment Tharagavverug
weakened. All that day Leothric drove him with his
stick, and at night both held their ground; and when
the dawn of the third day was come the heart of
Tharagavverug beat slower and fainter. It was as though
a tired man was ringing a bell. Once Tharagavverug
nearly seized a frog, but Leothric snatched it away just
in time. Towards noon the dragon-crocodile lay still
for a long while, and Leothric stood near him and
leaned on his trusty stick. He was very tired and sleep-
less, but had more leisure now for eating his provisions.
With Tharagavverug the end was coming fast, and in
the afternoon his breath came hoarsely, rasping in his
throat. It was as the sound of many huntsmen blowing
blasts on horns, and towards evening his breath came
faster but fainter, like the sound of a hunt going

furious to the distance and dying away, and he made desperate rushes towards the village; but Leothric still leapt about him, battering his leaden nose. Scarce audible now at all was the sound of his heart: it was like a church bell tolling beyond hills for the death of someone unknown and far away. Then the sun set and flamed in the village windows, and a chill went over the world, and in some small garden a woman sang; and Tharagavverug lifted up his head and starved, and his life went from his invulnerable body, and Leothric lay down beside him and slept. And later in the starlight the villagers came out and carried Leothric, sleeping, to the village, all praising bin in whispers as they went. They laid him down upon a couch in a house, and danced outside in silence, without psaltery or cymbal. And then next day, rejoicing, to Allathurion they hauled the dragon-crocodile. And Leothric went with them, holding his battered staff; and a tall, broad man, who was smith of Allathurion, made a great furnace, and melted Tharagavverug away till only Sacnoth was left, gleaming among the ashes. Then he took one of the small eyes that had been chiseled out, and filed an edge on Sacnoth, and gradually the steel eye wore away facet by facet, but ere it was quite gone it had sharpened redoubtable Sacnoth. But the other eye they set in the butt of the hilt, and it gleamed there bluely.

And that night Leothric arose in the dark and took the sword, and went westwards to find Gaznak; and he went through the dark forest till the dawn, and all the morning and till the afternoon. But in the afternoon he came into the open and saw in the midst of The Land Where No Man Goeth the fortress of Gaznak, mountainous before him, little more than a mile away.

And Leothric saw that the land was marsh and desolate. And the fortress went up all white out of it, with many buttresses, and was broad below but narrowed higher up, and was full of gleaming windows with the light upon them. And near the top of it a few white clouds were floating, but above them some of its pinnacles reappeared. Then Leothric advanced into the marshes, and the eye of Tharagavverug looked out warily from the hilt of Sacnoth; for Tharagavverug had known the marshes well, and the sword nudged Leothric to the right or pulled him to the left away from the dangerous places, and so brought him safely to the fortress walls.

And in the wall stood doors like precipices of steel, all studded with boulders of iron, and above every window were terrible gargoyles of stone; and the name of the fortress shone on the wall, writ large in letters of brass: "The Fortress Unvanquishable, Save For Sacnoth."

Then Leothric drew and revealed Sacnoth, and all the gargoyles grinned, and the grin went flickering from face to face right up into the cloud-abiding gables.

And when Sacnoth was revealed and all the gargoyles grinned, it was like the moonlight emerging from a cloud to look for the first time upon a field of blood, and passing swiftly over the wet faces of the slain that lie together in the horrible night. Then Leothric advanced towards a door, and it was mightier than the marble quarry, Sacremona, from which old men cut enormous slabs to build the Abbey of the Holy Tears. Day after day they wrenched out the very ribs of the hill until the Abbey was builded, and it was more beautiful than anything in stone. Then the priests blessed Sacremona, and it had rest, and no more stone was ever taken from it to build the houses of men. And the hill stood looking southwards lonely in the sunlight, defaced by that mighty scar. So vast was the door of steel. And the name of the door was The Porte Resonant, the Way of Egress for War.

Then Leothric smote upon the Porte Resonant with Sacnoth, and the echo of Sacnoth went ringing through the halls, and all the dragons in the fortress barked. And when the baying of the remotest dragon had faintly joined in the tumult, a window opened far up among the clouds below the twilit gables, and a woman screamed, and far away in Hell her father heard her and knew that her doom was come.

And Leothric went on smiting terribly with Sacnoth, and the grey steel of the Porte Resonant, the Way of Egress for War, that was tempered to resist the swords of the world, came away in ringing slices.

Then Leothric, holding Sacnoth in his hand, went in through the hole that he had hewn in the door, and came into the unlit, cavernous hall.

An elephant fled trumpeting. And Leothric stood still, holding Sacnoth. When the sound of the feet of the elephant had died away in remoter corridors, nothing more stirred, and the cavernous hall was still.

Presently the darkness of the distant halls became musical with the sound of bells, all coming nearer and nearer.

Still Leothric waited in the dark, and the bells rang louder and louder, echoing through the halls, and there appeared a procession of men on camels riding two by two from the interior of the fortress, and they were armed with scimitars of Assyrian make and were all clad with mail, and chain-mail hung from their helmets about their faces, and flapped as the camels moved. And they all halted before Leothric in the cavernous hall, and the camel bells clanged and stopped. And the leader said to Leothric:

"The Lord Gaznak has desired to see you die before him. Be pleased to come with us, and we can discourse

by the way of the manner in which the Lord Gaznak
has desired to see you die."

And as he said this he unwound a chain of iron that
was coiled upon his saddle, and Leothric answered:

"I would fain go with you, for I am come to slay
Gaznak."

Then all the camel-guard of Gaznak laughed hide-
ously, disturbing the vampires that were asleep in the
measureless vault of the roof And the leader said:

"The Lord Gaznak is immortal, save for Sacnoth,
and weareth armor that is proof even against Sacnoth
himself and hath a sword the second most terrible in
the world."

Then Leothric said: "I am the Lord of the sword
Sacnoth."

And he advanced towards the camel-guard of
Gaznak, and Sacnoth lifted up and down in his hand
as though stirred by an exultant pulse. Then the camel-
guard of Gaznak fled, and the riders leaned forward
and smote their camels with whips, and they went away
with a great clamor of bells through colonnades and
corridors and vaulted halls, and scattered into the
inner darknesses of the fortress. When the last sound
of them had died away, Leothric was in doubt which
way to go, for the camel-guard was dispersed in many
directions, so he went straight on till he came to a great
stairway in the midst of the hall. Then Leothric set his
foot in the middle of a wide step, and climbed steadily
up the stairway for five minutes. Little light was there
in the great hall through which Leothric ascended, for
it only entered through arrow slits here and there, and
in the world outside evening was waning fast. The
stairway led up to two folding doors, and they stood
a little ajar, and through the crack Leothric entered and
tried to continue straight on, but could get no further,
for the whole room seemed to be full of festoons of

ropes which swung from wall to wall and were looped and draped from the ceiling. The whole chamber was thick and black with them. They were soft and light to the touch, like fine silk, but Leothric was unable to break anyone of them, and though they swung away from him as he pressed forward, yet by the time he had gone three yards they were all about him like a heavy cloak. Then Leothric stepped back and drew Sacnoth, and Sacnoth divided the ropes without a sound, and without a sound the severed pieces fell to the floor. Leothric went forward slowly, moving Sacnoth in front of him up and down as he went. When he was come into the middle of the chamber, suddenly, as he parted with Sacnoth a great hammock of strands, he saw a spider before him that was larger than a ram, and the spider looked at him with eyes that were little, but in which there was much sin, and said:

"Who are you that spoil the labor of years all done to the honor of Satan?"

And Leothric answered: "I am Leothric, son of Lorendiac."

And the spider said: "I will make a rope at once to hang you with."

Then Leothric parted another bunch of strands, and came nearer to the spider as he sat making his rope, and the spider, looking up from his work, said: "What is that sword which is able to sever my ropes?"

And Leothric said: "It is Sacnoth."

Thereat the black hair that hung over the face of the spider parted to left and right, and the spider frowned: then the hair fell back into its place, and hid everything except the sin of the little eyes which went on gleaming lustfully in the dark. But before Leothric could reach him, he climbed away with his hands, going up by one of his ropes to a lofty rafter, and there sat, growling. But clearing his way with Sacnoth, Leothric passed through the chamber, and came to the further door; and the door being shut, and the handle far up out of his reach, he hewed his way through it with Sacnoth in the same way as he had through the Porte Resonant, the Way of Egress for War. And so Leothric came into a well-lit chamber, where Queens and Princes were banqueting together, all at a great table; and thousands of candles were glowing all about, and their light shone in the wine that the Princes drank and on the huge gold candelabra, and the royal faces were irradiant with the glow, and the white tablecloth and the silver plates and the jewels in the hair of the Queens, each jewel having a historian all to itself who wrote no other chronicles all his days. Between the table and the door there stood two hundred footmen in two rows of one hundred facing one another. Nobody looked at Leothric as he entered through the hole in the door, but one of the Princes asked a question of a footman, and the question was passed from mouth to mouth by all the hundred footmen till it came to the last one nearest Leothric; and he said to Leothric, without looking at him:

"What do you seek here?"

And Leothric answered: "I seek to slay Gaznak."

And footman to footman repeated all the way to the table: "He seeks to slay Gaznak."

And another question came down the line of footmen: "What is your name?"

And the line that stood opposite took his answer back.

Then one of the Princes said: "Take him away where we shall not hear his screams."

And footman repeated it to footman till it came to the last two, and they advanced to seize Leothric.

Then Leothric showed to them his sword, saying, "This is Sacnoth," and both of them said to the man nearest: "It is Sacnoth," then screamed and fled away.

And two by two, all up the double line, footman to footman repeated: "It is Sacnoth," then screamed and fled, till the last two gave the message to the table, and all the rest had gone. Hurriedly then arose the Queens and Princes, and fled out of the chamber. And the goodly table, when they were all gone, looked small and disorderly and awry. And to Leothric, pondering in the desolate chamber by what door he should pass onwards, there came from far away the sounds of music, and he knew that it was the magical musicians playing to Gaznak while he slept.

Then Leothric, walking towards the distant music, passed out by the door opposite to the one through which he had cloven his entrance, and so passed into a chamber vast as the other, in which were many women, weirdly beautiful. And they all asked him of his quest, and when they heard that it was to slay Gaznak, they all besought him to tarry among them, saying that Gaznak was immortal, save for Sacnoth, and also that they had need of a knight to protect them from the wolves that rushed round and round the wainscot all the night and sometimes broke in upon them through the moldering oak. Perhaps Leothric had been tempted to tarry had they been human women, for theirs was a strange beauty, but he perceived that instead of eyes they had little flames that flickered in their sockets, and knew them to be the fevered dreams of Gaznak. Therefore he said:

"I have a business with Gaznak and with Sacnoth," and passed on through the chamber.

And at the name of Sacnoth those women screamed, and the flames of their eyes sank low and dwindled to sparks.

And Leothric left them, and, hewing with Sacnoth, passed through the further door.

Outside he felt the night air on his face, and found that he stood upon a narrow way between two abysses. To left and right of him, as far as he could see, the walls of the fortress ended in a profound precipice, though the roof still stretched above him; and before him lay the two abysses full of stars, for they cut their way through the whole Earth and revealed the under sky; and threading its course between them went the way, and it sloped upward and its sides were sheer. And beyond the abysses, where the way led up to the further chambers of the fortress, Leothric heard the musicians playing their magical tune. So he stepped on to the way, which was scarcely a stride in width, and moved along it holding Sacnoth naked. And to and fro beneath him in each abyss whirred the wings of vampires passing up and down, all giving praise to Satan as they flew. Presently he perceived the dragon Thok lying upon the way, pretending to sleep, and his tail hung down into one of the abysses.

And Leothric went towards him, and when he was quite close Thok rushed at Leothric.

And he smote deep with Sacnoth, and Thok tumbled into the abyss, screaming, and his limbs made a whirring in the darkness as he fell, and he fell till his scream sounded no louder than a whistle and then could be heard no more. Once or twice Leothric saw a star blink for an instant and reappear again, and this momentary eclipse of a few stars was all that remained in the world of the body of Thok. And Lunk, the brother of Thok, who had lain a little behind him, saw that this must be Sacnoth and fled lumbering away. And all the while that he walked between the abysses, the mighty vault of the roof of the fortress still stretched over Leothric's head, all filled with gloom. Now, when the further side of the abyss came into view, Leothric saw a chamber that opened with innumerable arches upon the twin abysses, and the pillars of the arches went away into the distance and vanished in the gloom to left and right.

Far down the dim precipice on which the pillars stood he could see windows small and closely barred, and between the bars there showed at moments, and disappeared again, things that I shall not speak of.

There was no light here except for the great Southern stars that shone below the abysses, and here and there in the chamber through the arches lights that moved furtively without the sound of footfall.

Then Leothric stepped from the way, and entered the great chamber.

Even to himself he seemed but a tiny dwarf as he walked under one of those colossal arches.

The last faint light of evening flickered through a window painted in somber colors commemorating the achievements of Satan upon Earth. High up in the wall the window stood, and the streaming lights of candles lower down moved stealthily away.

Other light there was none, save for a faint blue glow from the steel eye of Tharagavverug that peered restlessly about it from the hilt of Sacnoth.

Heavily in the chamber hung the clammy odor of a large and deadly beast.

Leothric moved forward slowly with the blade of Sacnoth in front of him feeling for a foe, and the eye in the hilt of it looking out behind.

Nothing stirred.

If anything lurked behind the pillars of the colonnade that held aloft the roof it neither breathed nor moved.

The music of the magical musicians sounded from very near.

Suddenly the great doors on the far side of the chamber opened to left and right. For some moments Leothric saw nothing move, and waited clutching Sacnoth. Then Wong Bongerok came towards him, breathing.

This was the last and faithfullest guard of Gaznak, and came from slobbering just now his master's hand.

More as a child than a dragon was Gaznak wont to treat him, giving him often in his fingers tender pieces of man all smoking from his table.

Long and low was Wong Bongerok, and subtle about the eyes, and he came breathing malice against Leothric out of his faithful breast, and behind him roared the armory of his tail, as when sailors drag the cable of the anchor all rattling down the deck.

And well Wong Bongerok knew that he now faced Sacnoth, for it had been his wont to prophesy quietly to himself for many years as he lay curled at the feet of Gaznak.

And Leothric stepped forward into the blast of his breath, and lifted Sacnoth to strike.

But when Sacnoth was lifted up, the eye of Tharagavverug in the butt of the hilt beheld the dragon and perceived his subtlety.

For he opened his mouth wide, and revealed to Leothric the ranks of his saber teeth, and his leather gums flapped upwards. But while Leothric made to smite at his head, he shot forward scorpion-wise over his head the length of his armored tail. All this the eye perceived in the hilt of Sacnoth, who smote suddenly sideways. Not with the edge smote Sacnoth, for, had he done so, the severed end of the tail had still come hurtling on, as some pine tree that the avalanche has hurled point foremost from the cliff right through the broad breast of some mountaineer. So had Leothric been transfixed; but Sacnoth smote sideways with the flat of his blade, and sent the tail whizzing over Leothric's left shoulder; and it rasped upon his armor as it went, and left a groove upon it. Sideways then Leothric smote the foiled tail of Wong Bongerok, and Sacnoth parried, and the tail went shrieking up the blade and over Leothric's head. Then Leothric and Wong Bongerok fought sword to tooth, and the sword smote as only Sacnoth can, and the evil faithful life of Wong Bongerok the dragon went out through the wide wound.

Then Leothric walked on past that dead monster, and the armored body still quivered a little. And for a while it was like all the plowshares in a county working together in one field behind tired and struggling horses; then the quivering ceased, and Wong Bongerok lay still to rust.

And Leothric went on to the open gates, and Sacnoth dripped quietly along the floor.

By the open gates through which Wong Bongerok had entered, Leothric came into a corridor echoing with music. This was the first place from which Leothric could see anything above his head, for hitherto the roof had ascended to mountainous heights and had stretched indistinct in the gloom. But along the narrow corridor hung huge bells low and near to his head, and the width of each brazen bell was from wall to wall, and they were one behind the other. And as he passed under each the bell uttered, and its voice was mournful and deep, like to the voice of a bell speaking to a man for the last time when he is newly dead. Each bell uttered once as Leothric came under it, and their voices sounded solemnly and wide apart at ceremonious intervals. For if he walked slow, these bells came closer together, and when he walked swiftly they moved further apart. And the echoes of each bell tolling above his head went on before him whispering to the others. Once when he stopped they all jangled angrily till he went on again.

Between these slow and boding notes came the sound of the magical musicians. They were playing a dirge now very mournfully.

And at last Leothric came to the end of the Corridor of the Bells, and beheld there a small black door. And all the corridor behind him was full of the echoes of the tolling, and they all muttered to one another about the ceremony; and the dirge of the musicians came floating slowly through them like a procession of foreign elaborate guests, and all of them boded ill to Leothric.

The black door opened at once to the hand of Leothric, and he found himself in the open air in a wide court paved with marble. High over it shone the moon, summoned there by the hand of Gaznak.

There Gaznak slept, and around him sat his magical musicians, all playing upon strings. And even sleeping Gaznak was clad in armor, and only his wrists and face and neck were bare.

But the marvel of that place was the dreams of Gaznak; for beyond the wide court slept a dark abyss, and into the abyss there poured a white cascade of marble stairways, and widened out below into terraces and balconies with fair white statues on them, and descended again in a wide stairway, and came to lower terraces in the dark, where swart uncertain shapes went to and fro. All these were the dreams of Gaznak, and issued from his mind, and, becoming marble, passed over the edge of the abyss as the musicians played. And all the while out of the mind of Gaznak, lulled by that strange music, went spires and pinnacles beautiful and slender, ever ascending skywards. And the marble dreams moved slow in time to the music. When the bells tolled and the musicians played their dirge, ugly gargoyles came out suddenly all over the spires and pinnacles, and great shadows passed swiftly down the steps amid terraces, and there was hurried whispering in the abyss.

When Leothric stepped from the black door, Gaznak opened his eyes. He looked neither to left nor right, but stood up at once facing Leothric.

Then the magicians played a deathspell on their strings, and there arose a humming along the blade of Sacnoth as he turned the spell aside. When Leothric dropped not down, and they heard the humming of Sacnoth, the magicians arose and fled, all wailing, as they went, upon their strings.

Then Gaznak drew out screaming from its sheath the sword that was the mightiest in the world except for Sacnoth, and slowly walked towards Leothric; and he smiled as he walked, although his own dreams had foretold his doom. And when Leothric and Gaznak came together, each looked at each, and neither spoke a word; but they smote both at once, and their swords met, and each sword knew the other and from whence he came. And whenever the sword of Gaznak smote on the blade of Sacnoth it rebounded gleaming, as hail from off slated roofs; but whenever it fell upon the armor of Leothric, it stripped it off in sheets. And upon Gaznak's armor Sacnoth fell oft and furiously, but ever he came back snarling, leaving no mark behind, and as Gaznak fought he held his left hand hovering close over his head. Presently Leothric smote fair and fiercely at his enemy's neck, but Gaznak, clutching his own head by the hair, lifted it high aloft, and Sacnoth went cleaving through an empty space. Then Gaznak replaced his head upon his neck, and all the while fought nimbly with his sword; and again and again Leothric swept with Sacnoth at Gaznak's bearded neck, and ever the left hand of Gaznak was quicker than the stroke, and the head went up and the sword rushed vainly under it.

And the ringing fight went on till Leothric's armor lay all round him on the floor and the marble was splashed with his blood, and the sword of Gaznak was notched like a saw from meeting the blade of Sacnoth. Still Gaznak stood unwounded and smiling still.

At last Leothric looked at the throat of Gaznak and aimed with Sacnoth, and again Gaznak lifted his head by the hair; but not at his throat flew Sacnoth, for Leothric struck instead at the lifted hand, and through the wrist of it went Sacnoth whirring, as a scythe goes through the stem of a single flower.

And bleeding, the severed hand fell to the floor; and at once blood spurted from the shoulders of Gaznak and dripped from the fallen head, and the tall pinnacles went down into the earth, and the wide fair terraces all rolled away, and the court was gone like the dew, and a wind came and the colonnades drifted thence, and all the colossal halls of Gaznak fell. And the abysses closed up suddenly as the mouth of a man who, having told a tale, will forever speak no more.

Then Leothric looked around him in the marshes where the night mist was passing away, and there was no fortress nor sound of dragon or mortal, only beside him lay an old man, wizened and evil and dead, whose head and hand were severed from his body.

And gradually over the wide lands the dawn was coming up, and ever growing in beauty as it came, like to the peal of an organ played by a master's hand, growing louder and lovelier as the soul of the master warms, and at last giving praise with all its mighty voice.

Then the birds sang, and Leothric went homeward, and left the marshes and came to the dark wood, and the light of the dawn ascending lit him upon his way.

And into Allathurion he came ere noon, and with him brought the evil wizened head, and the people rejoiced, and their nights of trouble ceased.

*T*his is the tale of the vanquishing of The Fortress Unvanquishable, Save For Sacnoth, and of its passing away, as it is told and believed by those who love the mystic days of old.

Others have said, and vainly claim to prove, that a fever came to Allathurion, and went away; and that this same fever drove Leothric into the marshes by night, and made him dream there and act violently with a sword.

And others again say that there hath been no town of Allathurion, and that Leothric never lived.

Peace to them. The gardener hath gathered up this autumn's leaves. Who shall see them again, or who wot of them? And who shall say what bath befallen in the days of long ago?

# The Lord of Cities

*I* came one day upon a road that wandered so aim-
lessly that it was suited to my mood, so I followed it,
and it led me presently among deep woods. Somewhere
in the midst of them Autumn held his court, sitting
wreathed with gorgeous garlands; and it was the day
before his annual festival of the Dance of Leaves, the
courtly festival upon which hungry Winter rushes
moblike, and there arise the furious cries of the North
Wind triumphing, and all the splendor and grace of
the woods is gone, and Autumn flees away, discrowned
and forgotten, and never again returns. Other
Autumns arise, other Autumns, and fall before other
Winters. A road led away to the left, but my road went
straight on. The road to the left had a trodden appearance; there were wheel tracks on it, and it seemed the
correct way to take. It looked as if no one could have
any business with the road that led straight on and up
the hill. Therefore I went straight on and up the hill;
and here and there on the road grew blades of grass
undisturbed in the repose and hush that the road had
earned from going up and down the world; for you
can go by this road, as you can go by all roads, to

London, to Lincoln, to the North of Scotland, to the West of Wales, and to Wrellisford where roads end. Presently the woods ended, and I came to the open fields and at the same moment to the top of the hill, and saw the high places of Somerset and the downs of Wilts spread out along the horizon. Suddenly I saw underneath me the village of Wrellisford, with no sound in its street but the voice of the Wrellis roaring as he tumbled over a weir above the village. So I followed my road down over the crest of the hill, and the road became more languid as I descended, and less and less concerned with the cares of a highway. Here a spring broke out in the middle of it, and here another; the road never heeded. A stream ran right across it, still it straggled on. Suddenly it gave up the minimum property that a road should possess, and, renouncing its connection with High Streets, its lineage of Piccadilly, shrank to one side and became an unpretentious footpath. Then it led me to the old bridge over the stream, and thus I came to Wrellisford, and found after traveling in many lands a village with no wheel tracks in its street. On the other side of the bridge, my friend the road struggled a few yards up a grassy slope, and there ceased. Over all the village hung a great stillness, with the roar of the Wrellis cutting right across it, and there came occasionally the bark of a dog that kept watch over the broken stillness and over the sanctity of that untraveled road. That terrible and wasting fever that, unlike so many plagues, comes not from the East but from the West, the fever of hurry, had not come here — only the Wrellis hurried on his eternal quest, but it was a calm and placid hurry that gave one time for song. It was in the early afternoon, and nobody was about. Either they worked beyond the mysterious valley that nursed Wrellisford and hid it from the world, or else they secluded themselves within their old-time houses that were roofed with tiles of stone. I sat down upon the old stone bridge and watched the Wrellis, who seemed to me to be the only traveler that came from far away into this village where roads end, and passed on beyond it. And yet the Wrellis comes singing out of eternity, and tarries for a very little while in the village where roads end, and passes on into eternity again; and so surely do all that dwell in Wrellisford. I wondered as I leaned upon the bridge in what place the Wrellis would first find the sea, whether as he wound idly through meadows on his long quest he would suddenly behold him, and, leaping down over some rocky cliff, take to him at once the message of the hills. Or whether, widening slowly into some grand and tidal estuary, he would take his waste of waters to the sea and the might of the river should meet with the might of the waves, like to two Emperors clad in gleaming mail meeting midway between two hosts of war; and the little Wrellis would become a haven for returning ships and a setting-out place for adventurous men.

A little beyond the bridge there stood an old mill with a ruined roof, and a small branch of the Wrellis rushed through its emptiness shouting, like a boy playing alone in a corridor of some desolate house. The mill-wheel was gone, but there lay there still great bars and wheels and cogs, the bones of some dead industry. I know not what industry was once lord in that house, I know not what retinue of workers mourns him now; I only know who is lord there today in all those empty chambers. For as soon as I entered, I saw a whole wall draped with his marvelous black tapestry, without price because inimitable and too delicate to pass from hand to hand among merchants. I looked at the wonderful complexity of its infinite threads, my finger sank into it for more than an inch without feeling the touch; so black it was and so carefully wrought, somberly covering the whole of the wall, that it might have been worked to commemorate the deaths of all that ever lived there, as indeed it was. I looked through a hole in the wall into an inner chamber where a worn-out driving band went among many wheels, and there this priceless inimitable stuff not merely clothed the walls but hung from bars and ceiling in beautiful draperies, in marvelous festoons. Nothing was ugly in this desolate house, for the busy artist's soul of its present lord had beautified everything in its desolation. It was the unmistakable work of the spider, in whose house I was, and the house was utterly desolate but for him, and silent but for the roar of the Wrellis and the shout of the little stream. Then I turned homewards; and as I went up and over the hill and lost the sight of the village, I saw the road whiten and harden and gradually broaden out till the tracks of wheels appeared; and it went afar to take the young men of Wrellisford into the wide ways of the earth — to the new West and the mysterious East, and into the troubled South.

And that night, when the house was still and sleep was far off, hushing hamlets and giving ease to cities, my fancy wandered up that aimless road and came suddenly to Wrellisford. And it seemed to me that the traveling of so many people for so many years between Wrellisford and John o' Groat's, talking to one another as they went or muttering alone, had given the road a voice. And it seemed to me that night that the road spoke to the river by Wrellisford bridge, speaking with the voice of many pilgrims. And the road said to the river: "I rest here. How is it with you?"

And the river, who is always speaking, said: "I rest nowhere from doing the Work of the World. I carry the murmur of inner lands to the sea, and to the abysses voices of the hills."

"It is I," said the road, "that do the Work of the World, and take from city to city the rumor of each. There is nothing higher than Man and the making of cities. What do you do for Man?"

And the river said: "Beauty and song are higher than Man. I carry the news seaward of the first song of the thrush after the furious retreat of winter northward, and the first timid anemone learns from me that she is safe and that spring has truly come. Oh but the song of all the birds in spring is more beautiful than Man, and the first coming of the hyacinth more delectable than his face! When spring is fallen upon the days of summer, I carry away with mournful joy at night petal by petal the rhododendron's bloom. No lit procession of purple kings is nigh so fair as that. No beautiful death of well-beloved men hath such a glory of forlornness. And I bear far away the pink and white petals of the apple-blossom's youth when the laborious time comes for his work in the world and for the bearing of apples. And I am robed each day and every night anew with the beauty of heaven, and I make lovely visions of the trees. But Man! What is Man? In the ancient parliament of the elder hills, when the grey ones speak together, they say naught of Man, but concern themselves only with their brethren the stars. Or when they wrap themselves in purple cloaks at evening, they lament some old irreparable wrong, or, uttering some mountain hymn, all mourn the set of sun."

"Your beauty," said the road, "and the beauty of the sky, and of the rhododendron blossom and of spring, live only in the mind of Man, and except in the mind of Man the mountains have no voices. Nothing is beautiful that has not been seen by Man's eye. Or if

your rhododendron blossom was beautiful for a moment, it soon withered and was drowned, and spring
soon passes away; beauty can only live on in the mind
of Man. I bring thought into the mind of Man swiftly
from distant places every day. I know the Telegraph —
I know him well; he and I have walked for hundreds
of miles together. There is no work in the world except
for Man and the making of his cities. I take wares to
and fro from city to city."

"My little stream in the field there," said the river,
"used to make wares in that house for awhile once."

"Ah," said the road, "I remember, but I brought
cheaper ones from distant cities. Nothing is of any
importance but making cities for Man."

"I know so little about him," said the river, "but I
have a great deal of work to do — I have all this water
to send down to the sea; and then tomorrow or next
day all the leaves of Autumn will be coming this way.
It will be very beautiful. The sea is a very, very wonderful place. I know all about it; I have heard shepherd
boys singing of it, and sometimes before a storm the
gulls come up. It is a place all blue and shining and
full of pearls, and has in it coral islands and isles of
spice, and storms and galleons and the bones of Drake.
The sea is much greater than Man. When I come to
the sea, he will know that I have worked well for him.
But I must hurry, for I have much to do. This bridge
delays me a little; some day I will carry it away."

"Oh, you must not do that," said the road.

"Oh, not for a long time," said the river. "Some
centuries perhaps — and I have much to do besides.
There is my song to sing, for instance, and that alone
is more beautiful than any noise that Man makes."

"All work is for Man," said the road, "and for the
building of cities. There is no beauty or romance or
mystery in the sea except for the men that sail abroad

upon it, and for those that stay at home and dream of them. As for your song, it rings night and morning, year in, year out, in the ears of men that are born in Wrellisford; at night it is part of their dreams, at morning it is the voice of day, and so it becomes part of their souls. But the song is not beautiful in itself. I take these men with your song in their souls up over the edge of the valley and a long way off beyond, and I am a strong and dusty road up there, and they go with your song in their souls and turn it into music and gladden cities. But nothing is the Work of the World except work for Man."

"I wish I was quite sure about the Work of the World," said the stream; "I wish I knew for certain for whom we work. I feel almost sure that it is for the sea. He is very great and beautiful. I think that there can be no greater master than the sea. I think that some day he may be so full of romance and mystery and sound of sheep bells and murmur of mist-hidden hills, which we streams shall have brought him, that there will be no more music or beauty left in the world, and all the world will end; and perhaps the streams shall gather at the last, we all together, to the sea. Or perhaps the sea will give us at the last unto each one his own again, giving back all that he has garnered in the years – the little petals of the apple-blossom and the mourned ones of the rhododendron, and our old visions of the trees and sky; so many memories have left the hills. But who may say? For who knows the tides of the sea?"

"Be sure that it is all for Man," said the road. "For Man and the making of cities."

Something had come near on utterly silent feet.

"Peace, peace!" it said. "You disturb the queenly night, who, having come into this valley, is a guest in my dark halls. Let us have an end to this discussion."

It was the spider who spoke.

"The Work of the World is the making of cities and palaces. But it is not for Man. What is Man? He only prepares my cities for me, and mellows them. All his works are ugly, his richest tapestries are coarse and clumsy. He is a noisy idler. He only protects me from mine enemy the wind; and the beautiful work in my cities, the curving outlines and the delicate weavings, is all mine. Ten years to a hundred it takes to build a city, for five or six hundred more it mellows, and is prepared for me; then I inhabit it, and hide away all that is ugly, and draw beautiful lines about it to and fro. There is nothing so beautiful as cities and palaces; they are the loveliest places in the world, because they are the stillest, and so most like the stars. They are noisy at first, for a little, before I come to them; they have ugly comers not yet rounded off, and coarse tapestries, and then they become ready for me and my exquisite work, and are quite silent and beautiful. And there I entertain the regal nights when they come there jeweled with stars, and all their train of silence, and regale them with costly dust. Already nods, in a city that I wot of, a lonely sentinel whose lords are dead, who grows too old and sleepy to drive away the gathering silence that infests the streets; tomorrow I go to see if he be still at his post. For me Babylon was built, and rocky Tyre; and still men build my cities! All the Work of the World is the making of cities, and all of them I inherit."

# The Doom of La Traviata

*E*vening stole up out of mysterious lands and came down on the streets of Paris, and the things of the day withdrew themselves and hid away, and the beautiful city was strangely altered, and with it the hearts of men. And with lights and music, and in silence and in the dark, the other life arose, the life that knows the night, and dark cats crept from the houses and moved to silent places, and dim streets became haunted with dusk shapes. At this hour in a mean house, near to the Moulin Rouge, La Traviata died; and her death was brought to her by her own sins, and not by the years of God. But the soul of La Traviata drifted blindly about the streets where she had sinned till it struck against the wall of Notre Dame de Paris. Thence it rushed upwards, as the sea mist when it beats against a cliff, and streamed away to Paradise, and was there judged. And it seemed to me, as I watched from my place of dreaming, when La Traviata came and stood before the seat of judgment, that clouds came rushing up from the far Paradisal hills and gathered together over the head of God, and became one black cloud; and the clouds moved swiftly as shadows of the night when a lantern is swung in the hand, and more and more clouds rushed up, and ever more and more, and, as they gathered, the cloud a little above the head of God became no larger, but only grew blacker and blacker. And the halos of the saints settled lower upon their heads and narrowed and became pale, and the singing of the choirs of the seraphim faltered and sunk low, and the converse of the blessed suddenly ceased. Then a stem look came into the face of God, so that the seraphim turned away and left Him, and the saints. Then God commanded, and seven great angels rose up slowly through the clouds that carpet Paradise, and there was pity on their faces, and their eyes were closed. Then God pronounced judgment, and the lights of Paradise went out, and the azure crystal windows that look towards the world, and the windows rouge and verd, became dark and colorless, and I saw no more. Presently the seven great angels came out by one of Heaven's gates and set their faces Hellwards, and four of them carried the young soul of La Traviata, and one of them went on before and one of them followed behind. These six trod with mighty strides the long and dusty road that is named the Way of the Damned, But the seventh flew above them all the way, and the light of the fires of Hell that was hidden from the six by the dust of that dreadful road flared on the feathers of his breast.

Presently the seven angels, as they swept Hellwards, uttered speech.

"She is very young," they said; and "She is very beautiful," they said; and they looked long at the soul of La Traviata, looking not at the stains of sin, but at that portion of her soul wherewith she had loved her sister a long while dead, who flitted now about an orchard on one of Heaven's hills with a low sunlight ever on her face, who communed daily with the saints when they passed that way going to bless the dead from Heaven's utmost edge. And as they looked long at the beauty of all that remained beautiful in her soul they said: "It is but a young soul;" and they would have taken her to one of Heaven's hills, and would there have given her a cymbal and a dulcimer, but they knew that the Paradisal gates were clamped and barred against La Traviata. And they would have taken her to a valley in the world where there were a great many flowers and a loud sound of streams, where birds were singing always and church bells rang on Sabbaths, only this they durst not do. So they swept onwards nearer and nearer Hell. But when they were come quite close and the glare was on their faces, and they saw the gates already divide and prepare to open outwards, they said: "Hell is a terrible city, and she is tired of cities;" then suddenly they dropped her by the side of the road, and wheeled and flew away. But into a great pink flower that was horrible and lovely grew the soul of La Traviata; and it had in it two eyes but no eyelids, and it stared constantly into the faces of all the passers-by that went along the dusty road to Hell; and the flower grew in the glare of the lights of Hell, and withered but could not die; only, one petal turned back towards the heavenly hills as an ivy leaf turns outwards to the day, and in the soft and silvery light of Paradise it withered not nor faded, but heard at times the commune of the saints coining murmuring from the distance, and sometimes caught the scent of orchards wafted from the heavenly hills, and felt a faint breeze cool it every evening at the hour when the saints to Heaven's edge went forth to bless the dead.

But the Lord arose with His sword, and scattered His disobedient angels as a thresher scatters chaff.

# On the Dry Land

Over the marshes hung the gorgeous night with all his wandering bands of nomad stars, and his whole host of still ones blinked and watched. Over the safe dry land to eastward, grey and cold, the first clear pallor of dawn was coming up above the heads of the immortal gods.

Then, as they neared at last the safety of the dry land, Love looked at the man whom he had led for so long through the marshes, and saw that his hair was white, for it was shining in the pallor of the dawn.

Then they stepped together on to the land, and the old man sat down weary on the grass, for they had wandered in the marshes for many years; and the light of the grey dawn widened above the heads of the gods.

And Love said to the old man, "I will leave you now."

And the old man made no answer, but wept softly.

Then Love was grieved in his little careless heart, and he said: "You must not be sorry that I go, nor yet regret me, nor care for me at all.

"I am a very foolish child, and was never kind to you, nor friendly. I never cared for your great thoughts, or for what was good in you, but perplexed you by leading you up and down the perilous marshes. And I was so heartless that, had you perished where I led you, it would have been naught to me, and I only stayed with you because you were good to play with.

"And I am cruel and altogether worthless and not such a one as any should be sorry for when I go, or one to be regretted, or even cared for at all."

And still the old man spoke not, but wept softly; and Love grieved bitterly in his kindly heart.

And Love said: "Because I am so small my strength has been concealed from you, and the evil that I have done. But my strength is great, and I have used it unjustly. Often I pushed you from the causeway through the marshes, and cared not if you drowned. Often I mocked you, and caused others to mock you. And often I led you among those that hated me, and laughed when they revenged themselves upon you.

"So weep not, for there is no kindness in my heart, but only murder and foolishness, and I am no companion for one so, wise as you, but am so frivolous and silly that I laughed at your noble dreams and hindered all your deeds. See now, you have found me out, and now you will send me away, and here you will live at ease, and, undisturbed, have noble dreams of the immortal gods.

"See now, here is dawn and safety, and there is darkness and peril."

Still the old man wept softly.

Then Love said: "Is it thus with you?" and his voice was grave now and quiet. "Are you so troubled? Old friend of so many years, there is grief in my heart for you. Old friend of perilous ventures, I must leave you now. But I will send my brother soon to you — my little brother Death. And he will come up out of the marshes to you, and will not forsake you, but will be true to you as I have not been true."

And dawn grew brighter over the immortal gods, and the old man smiled through his tears, which glistened wondrously in the increasing light. But Love went down to the night and to the marshes, looking backward over his shoulder as he went, and smiling beautifully about his eyes. And in the marshes whereunto he went, in the midst of the gorgeous night, and under the wandering bands of nomad stars, rose shouts of laughter and the sounds of the dance.

And after a while, with his face towards the morning, Death out of the marshes came up tall and beautiful, and with a faint smile shadowy on his lips, and lifted in his arms the lonely man, being gentle with him, and, murmuring with his low deep voice an ancient song, carried him to the morning, to the gods.